THE NIGHT I SHOT PETER WHITE

Paul J. Schwartz

iUniverse, Inc.
Bloomington

THE NIGHT I SHOT PETER WHITE

iUniverse books may be ordered through booksellers or by contacting:

iUniverse
1663 Liberty Drive
Bloomington, IN 47403
www.iuniverse.com
1-800-Authors (1-800-288-4677)

Because of the dynamic nature of the Internet, any web addresses or links contained in this book may have changed since publication and may no longer be valid. The views expressed in this work are solely those of the author and do not necessarily reflect the views of the publisher, and the publisher hereby disclaims any responsibility for them.

Any people depicted in stock imagery provided by Thinkstock are models, and such images are being used for illustrative purposes only.

Certain stock imagery © Thinkstock.

ISBN: 978-1-4759-6910-8 (sc)
ISBN: 978-1-4759-6911-5 (e)

Library of Congress Control Number: 2012924190

Printed in the United States of America

iUniverse rev. date: 1/03/2013

BANG! BANG!

Monday, November 30, 1998, 11:26 p.m.
Lakeside, Wisconsin

Squeeze the trigger, don't pull it. I knew the drill, had heard it on TV and in the movies, had read it in books, had heard it from Pete Atherton. But I still pulled the trigger, and I missed him of course at that distance (fifty yards).

He hardly reacted to the bullet that slammed into the cabinet behind him. Like the proverbial deer in the headlights, he froze. The second shell was already in the chamber. This time I squeezed the trigger. The sound of the second detonation was eerily different; it echoed and rang in my ears for what seemed like an interminable time. It surrounded and penetrated me. Through the scope, I saw the blood and everything else that splattered the cabinet as he went down. If he wasn't already dead, I knew the chances that the son of a bitch would ever teach math again were slim to none.

I carefully picked up the spent shells, put the rifle back in its case, and hiked three hundred yards back to the paved apartment parking lot at the nearby Forest Grove apartment complex where I had left my car. No one around, as I had expected. I had several times thought about what to do with the spent shells. I wasn't sure it mattered a whole lot. My final decision was to pack them into an empty cigarette package which I would dispose of during the night in the trash receptacle of a highway rest area, along with my shoes and the blood-spattered coat still in the trunk. For the moment, I slid the cigarette package with the shells under the driver's seat of my Subaru. I placed the gun case among the packed bags in the trunk. I would later bury it in a corner of Brown Creek State Park. My gun show purchased M-1 Carbine was popular enough to be virtually untraceable. The bullets could be traced to the gun if it was ever dug up, but the gun could not be traced to me. I calmly drove off on Route 114.

PART ONE: November 30, 1998

I woke up like always at six-thirty, had breakfast of cold cereal and orange juice, took a shower, put my already packed luggage, a spare pair of shoes, the shovel, and gun case into the trunk, and by seven-forty I was behind the wheel of the Subaru for the twenty minute drive to campus. My thoughts were surprisingly banal. I listened to Morning Edition for part of the drive, and, when I tired of the news of the House Judicial Committee's preparation for the Clinton impeachment hearings, turned to Lisa Nielson's classical music selections on KSJN. I listened with some attention to the local weather report, which confirmed what I had been hearing all weekend on TV and radio, and what I had read in the Minneapolis, Eau Claire, Wausau and Green Bay newspapers over several days. They predicted unusually mild temperatures, with daytime highs near sixty degrees. If the thirty percent chance of precipitation happened to materialize, it would be no threat to my plans.

I tried not to think about the rifle in my trunk, nestled among the luggage packed for a trip of several days I had no intention of taking, but which would, I thought, satisfy the police, if for any reason I was stopped (I had no intention of exceeding the speed limit or passing a yellow traffic light, but was determined to be prepared for any eventuality), in confirmation of my carefully prepared story about my plans for the opening of deer hunting season in Wisconsin on this the Monday after Thanksgiving. I had a Wisconsin hunting license ready to show. It occurred to me then, as I was driving through Saint Paul, that my unusually careful attention to speed limits, stop signs and traffic lights should begin then and there.

I of course thought a bit about Pete White. Thoughts of him had been poisoning my mind for . . . for how long exactly? Probably five years. During the first two years we had been colleagues, our relations

3

had been generally harmonious. It was only later, specifically around 1994, that animosity began to develop, leading eventually to my present intent to shoot a fatal bullet into his brain. I worked carefully on the wording of that sentence, avoiding the phrase "murderous hatred." It was nothing like that that inspired me that morning. My intention was of course murderous. But I felt no hatred. More about that later.

I had given some thought to the question where I would park my car that morning on campus. While I wanted in most ways to respect the routine that I had established, and not do anything different that might attract attention, I was a little concerned that if I parked as I usually did in my assigned spot behind Frederick Hall, I might get caught up in and delayed by the usual five p.m. traffic squeeze. I wanted to leave my office at five-ten, with the hope that by five-thirty I would be exiting the campus. I wanted there to be no chance that someone would later reflect that "Paul left early." Or "Paul seemed in a hurry." What I wanted was for people, if they noticed anything at all, to be able to say with perfect comfort, "Paul left the campus at the same time that he always did. He smiled and waved and wished me a good evening as we passed on campus. Oh, yes, he did mention that he was bringing home with him some reappointment folders, as his reports were due Wednesday." (In fact, I had already written those reports over the weekend, after changing the internal date in my laptop, so that Windows Explorer would record them as having been written that evening, Monday, November 30, 1998.)

So, I had decided to park in the East River Road Ramp using my occasional use contract; it was a good twelve minute walk to Frederick, but getting out from the ramp at five-thirty would be a lot easier. At eight sharp, I drove into a parking space on the second level, straightened my tie in the rear view mirror, grabbed my brief case from the passenger seat, and locked the car remotely as I walked briskly towards Frederick Hall.

Q: Dr. Steinman, my name is Elliot Cameron. I represent Peter White in a case brought against the University of Wisconsin. I have asked you to come here today to answer some questions about matters relating to the case. If I ask you anything that is not clear, that you don't understand, please tell me. Dr. Steinman, by whom are you employed?

A: The University of Saint Paul.

Q: In what capacity?

A: I am Dean of the College of Liberal Arts.

Q: How long have you been employed there?

A: Since July 8 of this year.

Q: And before that?

A: By the University of Wisconsin.

Q: In what capacity?

A: I was Associate Dean of the Lakeside Campus, starting in July, 1991.

Q: Where did you get your undergraduate degree?

A: Columbia University.

Q: Doctorate?

A: Ph.D. in Comparative Literature from Yale University.

Q: What did it mean to be Associate Dean at the Lakeside Campus of the University of Wisconsin?

A: I had responsibilities for faculty recruitment, development, promotion and tenure, and the annual evaluation process for salary recommendations. I also had supervisory responsibility for offices in the academic area such as the library, registrar's office, learning support, advising and academic computing.

Q: Do you know Peter White?

A: Yes.

Q: When did you first meet him?

A: In the late summer or early fall of 1991.

Q: Can you describe your relationship with Dr. White?

A: At first it was quite good. I remember the first issue that we had to deal with. It concerned scheduling for the fall semester of 1991. There was a disagreement between Dr. White and Dr. Chen over who would teach what course. It was my responsibility to try to get the parties to agree to a compromise solution. And I remember finding Dr. White flexible and understanding of the situation, and ultimately very cooperative.

Q: And did you continue to find him flexible and cooperative?

A: There were times later when I did not.

Q: When was the first time?

A: I can't remember that.

Q: What's the first time you remember?

A: The incident that comes to mind and sort of clouds out everything else was the fall of 1994, when it was a question of his teaching responsibilities for the spring semester of 1995. Were there incidents before that? I have a sense there were, but I can't remember any details of them.

Q: What was the incident in the spring of 1995?

A: We had been preparing the schedule for the spring semester of 1995, and Dr. White was not listed to teach any courses because it was my understanding that he was going to be on sabbatical leave beginning in January of 1995. Late in the fall semester, in early December 1994, I learned from a third party that he was not going to be going on sabbatical after all. So, I brought to his attention that he was not on the time schedule, and that we needed to assign him courses. He resisted that idea and did not want to be assigned any courses.

Q: Was there a resolution of this issue about teaching in the spring of 1995?

A: He failed to respond affirmatively to my requests that he accept responsibility for teaching courses in the spring semester, and so I assigned him two courses.

Q: Was that the end of it?

A: It certainly wasn't the end of it.

Q: When you say, "It certainly wasn't the end of it," what do you mean?

A: Ultimately, he did not teach the two courses that were assigned to him.

Q: Why not?

A: Well, first of all, on the Friday afternoon before spring classes were to begin on the following Monday, I had a phone message from an attorney that Dr. White, because of health reasons, would not be available to teach during the first two weeks of the semester. When those two weeks had elapsed, there was a subsequent call from the same attorney informing me that Dr. White would not be able to teach for the next two weeks. So, he missed the first four weeks of the semester, and his two courses were covered by an adjunct faculty member. Following his return in February, there was contentiousness surrounding the teaching of one of those courses, and I was forced to relieve him of the responsibility for that course, to protect the students.

Q: What was the contentiousness that led to your relieving Dr. White from responsibility for teaching one of his courses?

A: When he came back to campus and met with that class for the first time, he announced that a good number, eight or more, were not to continue in that course. He had looked at their work to that point, decided that they were not good enough to continue in his course, and urged them to go to the Advising Center to drop it. It came to my attention through the Advising Center that the students were all very upset.

7

Q: And then what did you do about that?

A: It was a Wednesday when I became aware of the situation, and the course was to meet again on the following Friday. I tried to call Dr. White, couldn't get him on the phone, and spoke instead to the Math Department secretary. I asked her to get a message to Dr. White, asking if it was all right if I met with him and the students during the class hour on Friday, to discuss the situation. The class was scheduled for two p.m.

Q: And then?

A: He agreed to that, and then that Friday morning, there was a fire on the roof of the science building. The fire department was called, and they came. The fire was quickly extinguished. It was discovered that the fire was the result of a short circuit in the ventilator fan on the roof, and the asphalt surrounding it had caught fire. The building was aired out, and declared safe for continued occupancy by students and staff.

Q: Who declared it safe?

A: The Business Officer of the campus.

Q: What else happened that day when you were going to meet with the class and there was a fire in the morning?

A: I walked over to the building, probably a little after noon, to check out its condition. I wanted to make sure that I had no reservations about the safety of the building. As I approached it, I noticed Dr. White with his coat on and a briefcase in his hand, leaving the building. He was walking towards the parking lot, and I asked him where he was going, and he said something about the fire. I told him the fire was out and the building was safe, and that it was very important that we meet with the students that day because they were very anxious.

He turned and walked back towards his office. I followed him to his office, trying to explain my concern for the students.

Q: Why did you follow him to his office?

A: Because I wanted to continue the conversation.

Q: Did he give you any clue that he did not want to continue the conversation?

A: Well, he closed the door in my face.

Q: What happened after that?

A: I went back to my office. Then, I went down to the classroom at about ten minutes to two. The students were there waiting for Dr. White.

Q: So what did you do when the students were there?

A: I talked to them. I tried to be reassuring because I knew they were anxious. I engaged them in conversation, trying to get more information, and at the same time be comforting.

    Finally, when it got to be five or ten after two, I told them I would go see what was keeping Dr. White. I walked down to his office. The door was open, and I saw him seated in his office on the phone, and I said, "Pete, the students are in the classroom, and we're waiting to begin this conversation." And I think he said, "I can't talk about this." And he closed the door again.

Q: And then what happened?

A: I walked back to the classroom and told them that Dr. White was on the phone, but I hoped he would come down to the classroom as soon as he finished his conversation. We waited around for another ten minutes or so, making small talk. Finally, I had to leave, as I had to be in Riverdale for a meeting that afternoon. So, I told the students they could leave, and we would try again on Monday to resolve the situation.

Q: I put before you what's marked as Plaintiff's Exhibit No. 25. Do you recognize that?

A: Yes.

Q: What is it?

A: A memo from me to Dr. White, dated February 23, 1995. After I relieved him of responsibility for teaching the

Math 110 course, he asked me to put in writing that I was relieving him of that responsibility.

Q: About a third of the way through the paragraph on the first page, there is a reference to Friday, February 10, which, I take it, is the day of the fire incident, right?

A: Yes.

Q: The last sentence on that page says, "You were apparently at that time on the phone complaining to offices at the Madison campus about my attempts to get you to meet your classroom responsibility." Upon what did you base that observation?

A: After I left the classroom, I stopped by my office before leaving campus for my three o'clock meeting in town. There was a note for me to call Janet Tremaine, who was Director of Human Resources for the Wisconsin College System. I felt I had to talk to her right away, because I thought it might have something to do with Dr. White.

   When I finally reached her, we had a conversation about the events of the day. She told me that she had been in conversation with Dr. White at various times during the day, and she pinpointed one of those times as being between two o'clock and ten minutes after two. And I said, "Oh, well, that's why he couldn't come to class at that time."

Q: Did she say what she was talking about with him?

A: The situation that was going on, on the campus, at that point.

Q: What did she say?

A: She said that Dr. White was accusing me of holding him hostage in a burning building. She used those very words.

Q: Looking again at the sentence I just read, it says that you believe he was complaining about your attempts to get him to meet his classroom responsibility. Upon what do you base that conclusion?

A: She said he accused me of holding him hostage in a burning building, whereas all I was trying to do was to get him to come to the classroom to meet with the class he was assigned to teach, in a building that was safe.

Q: So, your understanding that he was telling someone that he was held hostage in a burning building is complaining about your attempts to get him to meet his classroom responsibility.

A: That was mine.

Q: That's what that means?

A: That's what that means.

I had only three meetings scheduled for the day: IT Committee at ten, plus individual monthly one-on-one meetings with the chairs of the Theatre and English Departments in the afternoon. At about nine-thirty, while I was talking on the phone with one of my colleagues in the budget office, my secretary Sue Renquist came in with a note saying that Laura Higgins was on the other line. I whispered to her that she should tell Laura I would call her back after eleven, if that was OK with her. Laura was the University of Wisconsin lawyer working with us on the Peter White lawsuit.

After finishing my conversation with the budget office, I had time to answer some e-mails, approve a couple of on-line appointments of adjunct faculty for the spring semester, and get to Stanton Hall in time for the ten o'clock meeting of the IT Committee.

I had established a reputation for my performances at IT Committee meetings. It was often observed that I dozed off. It had become somewhat of a game among my colleagues to watch for the moment when my eyes definitively closed and my head sagged. Although many kidded me about that, others pointed out that even those who had the keenest interest in solving the many problems that plagued our IT system well into the 1990s – including occasional complete shutdowns – often turned glassy-eyed when the technical experts on the committee launched into overly detailed, and ultimately soporific explanations. At any rate, if my eyes closed during the meeting, no one would be surprised, business as usual in fact, and it might be helpful to me later to get through the long afternoon and night that awaited me. In the course of the meeting, I did in fact rise out of my stupor on a couple of occasions to make some useful observations and suggestions.

Continuation of the Deposition of Paul J. Steinman, PhD
September 3, 1998, 9:04 a.m.

Q: I am putting before you what is marked as Plaintiff's Exhibit No. 45. Tell me if you recognize that.

A: Yes.

Q: What is it?

A: It is a handwritten note from me to White, objecting to the fact that he had changed the time schedule without my approval.

Q: And insisting that his course meet three times a week as originally scheduled?

A: Yes.

Q: Why were you insisting that?

A: Changing the times of courses without going through proper channels can cause all kinds of problems, and my memory is that this one did.

Q: Did?

A: Did cause problems.

Q: What problems?

A: Student complaints.

Q: Let me show you Plaintiff's Exhibit No. 46. Do you recognize this?

A: I recognize this.

Q: What is it?

A: It is an e-mail from me to Dr. White, contemporary to the handwritten note, probably written the same day, elaborating further on the issue of the class change.

Q: Let's look at the second page of this document. Am I correct you wrote there, the last sentence, I quote, "I do hope that these issues will be resolved before

Friday and trust in your judgment to do what is best for our students."

A: Yes, I wrote that.

Q: You then trusted in Dr. White's judgment?

A: I do not know exactly what I was thinking when I wrote that.

Q: Do you mean you weren't thinking exactly what it says?

A: Sometimes one writes things with ulterior motives…

Q: Yes?

A: Period. End of sentence.

Q: At the Lakeside Campus are there not several academic departments represented?

A: Yes.

Q: And were there individuals designated as the local chairs of the departments?

A: Yes, program heads.

Q: Who selected them?

A: Me.

Q: Was the person designated generally the most senior person in the department?

A: Not necessarily, no.

Q: Can you think of any situation when it wasn't?

A: Yes, for example, the program head in electrical engineering technology is probably the youngest in that faculty who is also outranked by some of his departmental colleagues.

Q: What about math?

A: When I first arrived, it was Dr. White. While he was on leave for a semester, I selected Dr. Fleck to replace him, and he remained in that position for several semesters until I appointed Dr. Romanov. In neither case was Fleck or Romanov the ranking member of the department.

Q: Who was the ranking member of the department?

A: Dr. White.

Q: Did you consider making Dr. White the program head?

A: No, I did not.

Q: Why not?

A: I had lost faith in his ability to do that when he misled me about scheduling in the fall of 1994.

Q: Did you ever tell him that?

A: I am sure I did.

Q: Let me put before you Plaintiff's Exhibit 17, and tell me if you recognize that.

A: Yes.

Q: What is it?

A: A memo from me to Douglas Goldsmith, Chair of the Math Department at Madison, itemizing concerns about Dr. White's performance.

Q: Paragraph one says that Dr. White has consistently attempted to avoid teaching responsibility on the campus for the spring 1995 semester. What is the basis for that?

A: First, the fact that he did not put his name on the time schedule for the spring semester, even when he knew that he was not going on sabbatical. Secondly, he did not teach for the first four weeks of the semester, and then when he did teach, he tried to remove a large number of students from one of the two classes he was teaching, which led to my relieving him of responsibility for that course. Then he changed the meeting times of his remaining course to reduce the number of days per week that it was to meet. From my point of view, those were consistent attempts to avoid accepting teaching responsibilities.

Q: The first four weeks of the semester, why did he not teach?

A: We had information from his lawyer that he was unable to teach.

Q: For health reasons?

A: Yes.

Q: Were you ever skeptical of his illness?

A: Perhaps a little skeptical of his illness, yes.

Q: Why?

A: I had had a conversation with Dr. White about a week before his hospitalization, in early January. He called me at home and told me he didn't want to teach in the spring semester, and I told him that he had to. He indicated that he was tired and stressed, and I suggested to him a medical leave. That idea seemed interesting to him, and he asked me what I knew about that. I didn't know a lot, so I referred him to a Human Resources Officer.

Later I had a conversation with the Human Resources Officer to whom I had referred White. I asked her about the terms of a medical leave. She told me that a medical leave was without pay. We also discussed under what conditions a faculty member could have a leave with pay. She answered that there was no formal policy for that, but that it was a tradition within the academic community, at least within this academic community, that if a faculty member is absent due to illness for a short period of time, colleagues cover, and there is no loss of pay. I asked her what might be the normal length of such an informal medical leave, and she said two weeks. So, when I later heard from White's lawyer that he would be gone for two weeks, and I also knew that the Human Resources Officer had conveyed to Dr. White the same information she had given me, it made me a little skeptical.

Q: Who was Dr. Kadani?

A: A former campus faculty member who also filed a discrimination complaint.

Q: Was Dr. White in any way implicated in the Kadani case?

A: He was named in the complaint. Kadani listed a number of people who, in his opinion, had also suffered discrimination on the Lakeside Campus.

Q: What was your reaction?

A: This was fairly early in my appointment at Lakeside. I was puzzled, and wondered if these people had suffered discrimination on our campus. I was concerned about that.

Q: What did you do about your concern?

A: I asked Peter White if he had ever suffered discrimination on our campus.

Q: What did he say?

A: No.

Q: When was that?

A: I can't tell you exactly. It was after I had seen the documentation in the Kadani case. I think I asked him one day when we went to lunch together. I mentioned to him that I was surprised to see his name on this list of faculty who had suffered discrimination, and asked him if he ever felt discriminated against on our campus, and he said no.

Q: Did you ask him how his name got on the list.

A: No.

I got back to my office around eleven-fifteen, and tried to call Attorney Laura Higgins. I was aware that her focus at that point was to review point by point the depositions that I and my former Wisconsin colleagues had given in the course of the summer in the case of Peter R. White v. University of Wisconsin, and to try to mitigate the damage we had done. As Laura had gently put it to me, "Paul, you are a very nice man, and an able college administrator, but you are a terrible defense witness." My weakness was a tendency to say too much, to try to be helpful. I found myself wanting to explain myself, and thereby going well beyond the scope of the question I was answering, and opening cans of worms. At one point too in my deposition, I found myself agreeing with what seemed like a friendly assertion of the opposing counsel. That particular utterance had earned me a sharp poke and a glare from Laura that did not go unnoticed.

When I tried to call Laura back at eleven-fifteen, her secretary said she was tied up, and we agreed I would try her again around two p.m., when we both appeared to be free. In Laura's mind there was some urgency to our having several phone conversations and possibly even a face-to-face meeting, to prepare me for the jury trial which was scheduled to begin January 11 in the federal courthouse in Madison. I however was pretty sure that urgency would dissipate.

I made a few other phone calls, and was about to start on the peanut butter and jelly sandwich I had brought with me, when my boss, Provost Jeanne Hanratty, stuck her head in the door and invited me to go to lunch with her. I said sure, as long as I could be back in time for my scheduled two o'clock phone conversation with Laura. Jeanne had gotten to campus early that morning, and she had a parking space by the loading dock behind our building, so we took her Cherokee to the Dorset Inn for a leisurely lunch.

I had imagined she wanted to challenge some of the faculty reappointments I had already signed off on, so after we had ordered, I asked her if she had any reservations about my recommendations. She had no reservations at all, what she wanted to learn about was the University of Wisconsin lawsuit.

I think the President had probably asked her what she knew, and not knowing much, she thought she ought to question me about it. She assured me her curiosity was inspired by both professional and personal interest. She wanted to know if I had any real legal or financial exposure in the matter, and I was able to assure her that I was completely protected by my association with the University of Wisconsin. She then asked if I had any psychological exposure, would the loss of the suit be personally disturbing to me. There, the answer was a not so clear "no." I had to admit that I would hate to see the son of a bitch given any credibility for his claims of discrimination, that I knew that I had always behaved not only fairly towards him, but often with preferential treatment in anticipation of the easily foreseeable litigation that he was preparing. I had approved travel funds and equipment funds for him that I might not have approved for others.

But I also reassured her that White and the associated stresses had long before vanished from my rearview mirror when I had left the Lakeside position to come to Saint Paul as Dean. I told her I had left behind all the emotional fragility caused by the many stresses of my previous position at Lakeside, as well as by the recent death of my wife. And that was true. I was very happy at that moment in my professional life, and busy enough so that I had little time for grief.

She asked me to outline briefly the subject of the legal complaint, and I explained the component of his lawsuit that related directly to me. During the 1994-95 salary increase process at Lakeside, despite numerous reminders from me and others, White had failed to submit the annual activity report forms which form the factual basis for salary increase recommendations. In the absence of that report, I, like every other administrator involved in the process, had recommended no increase in salary for White. Ultimately, he did get a raise of about 1%, as the University had added that amount across the board at the end of the evaluation process. But White had sued, claiming that he did not receive the 3-4% he expected – and which he probably would have received if he had filed his report – because of discrimination on the basis of age and religion. White claimed that because he was a Mormon, he was often scorned, belittled and mistreated, and that the insulting salary increase was just another example of a continuous pattern of discrimination.

Jeanne seemed satisfied with my sanguineness. I thanked her for having hired me into the Dean's position at Saint Paul, thereby rescuing me from the quagmire of deteriorating morale at Lakeside, caused to a great extent by the poisonous presence of a crazy, discontented mathematician, who had turned other faculty against the administration, and who waged a campaign of shameless bullying against faculty colleagues, administrators, and even students who tried to stand up to him.

She was surprised that one man could have that severe an effect on the morale of an entire campus. I pointed out that the faculty was small and everyone knew everyone else. And that Peter White was particularly nasty. I gave her some examples. During one performance review, I had written a memo expressing expectations of him, which included the desire that he show more interest and willingness in meeting the needs of underprepared students, as that was an important component of the campus mission. He wrote back, with ccs to several university administrators, objecting that he had always been willing to work with underprepared students, and citing an example, something like, "Dean Steinman should remember that during the summer of 1993, I showed great interest, patience, and willingness in working with his son, a weak math student who was underprepared for the calculus course I taught that summer." It just wasn't true, but I swallowed my anger at the very personal and inappropriate jab, and ignored his response. I also told her about the adult technology student who had come into my office during the last year I was at the campus, and who told me with tears in his eyes, "Dean Steinman, I need to pass this calculus course, but I never will as long as Dr. White is the teacher. He only wants to teach students who are very good math students, and he told me I am not a very good math student."

And then finally I told her a story that Jim Sullivan had told me a couple of weeks after I had started working at the University of Saint Paul. Jim was a professor of English who had chaired the search committee that hired me. One day when we had gotten together for lunch, Jim revealed that during the search process he had received a call in his office from someone who identified himself as a faculty member at the Lakeside Campus of the University of Wisconsin, and said that he was calling to urge the University of Saint Paul not to hire Paul Steinman as dean, because Steinman was incompetent, dishonest and biased. I asked Sullivan if the caller perchance had a bit of a southwestern US accent, and Sullivan said that indeed he did. I was pretty sure that it was Peter White who had tried to sabotage my candidacy for the dean's position at Saint Paul.

Monday, November 30, 2 p.m.
Dean's Office, University of Saint Paul

I got back from lunch in plenty of time to call Attorney Laura Higgins at two, and she was there waiting for my call. After a brief exchange of pleasantries, she asked when we could schedule a meeting, either in person or by phone. She urged that we try to get together in person because she thought that would be more productive and efficient. I told her I wouldn't mind driving down to Madison on an afternoon of the following week, if the university would spring for an overnight hotel stay. We agreed on the following Wednesday, December 9. She asked me in the meantime to reread my deposition carefully, looking for examples of answers that went too generously beyond the intent of the question. She pointed out that Elliot Cameron, Pete White's attorney, liked to go fishing with his questions, and that I had on several occasions been an easy catch, volunteering information that was better left unrevealed, and sometimes undermining my credibility by questioning my own actions.

I understood the point. I assured her that while thoughtful people must be continuously questioning their statements and actions, I recognized that a jury might find that less admirable. She offered to find examples in my deposition for my edification and review prior to our meeting. We finally decided that she would e-mail a dozen or so references to page and line numbers that I might want to reread and reflect on before we had our discussion of how I might better address the same questions during the jury trial.

There was one glaring exchange that I knew she would highlight for me, the very one that had provoked the poke and the glare during the deposition. In an official memo to my supervisor, the Campus Dean, with ccs to the chair and associate chair of the University of Wisconsin Math Department and the Associate Dean of the Wisconsin College System, I had stated, "In the absence of any basis for a positive decision on a salary increase for Dr. White [referring to the absence of a faculty activity report], I recommend a zero increase."

The exchange concerning that memo had gone like this during the deposition:

```
Cameron:  Now, Dr. Steinman, do you recognize that in
          this memo you declare that you had no basis for
          a judgment of Dr. White's teaching during the
          previous year?
```

Steinman: Yes.

Cameron: Is it really true that you had no basis?

Steinman: Yes.

Cameron: Do you mean then that in your position as Associate Dean, as the campus officer responsible for assigning and evaluating Dr. White's teaching for the previous five years, you had no knowledge of what he had been teaching nor how effective he had been in that teaching?

Steinman: Oh, I see what you mean. The phrase, "absence of any basis," is overstated. Yes, I probably should have phrased that differently.

Afterwards, Laura had helped me understand that what I was willing to accept as a collegial exchange of points of view about the accuracy of something I had written, the kind of conversation which is routine in academic circles, could be made to appear to a jury of non-academics as an example of a guy not knowing what he was doing. I should instead have insisted feistily that I stood by my choice of words, that in academic administrative language, what I had written was accurate because unofficial communications and judgments of effectiveness were not acceptable bases for evaluation for the purpose of salary increase. The only acceptable basis would have been the evidence submitted with the faculty activity report. Laura assured me that answer would have ended the conversation. OK. Lesson learned.

At the conclusion of our phone conversation, Laura promised to e-mail me my hotel reservation and information about our meeting time and place on December 9. I thanked her for that, and told her that I was looking forward to our meeting. We both laughed.

From the Deposition of Peter White, PhD
October 3, 1998, 9:04 a.m.
By Mr. Fredericks

Q: Would you state your full name please.

A: Peter Richard White.

Q: Dr. White, can you explain to me why you are verbally abusive of staff who work at the Lakeside Campus?

A: Excuse me, could you repeat the question?

Q: Sure. Can you explain to me why you are consistently abusive of staff who work at the Lakeside Campus?

A: I don't think I have been.

Q: Your testimony is that you deny ever being verbally abusive of staff who work at the Lakeside Campus, correct, sir?

A: I do not recall being abusive to staff or anybody for that matter.

Q: Not just what you recall, your testimony is you deny being verbally abusive or hostile or non-collegial toward the staff who work at the Lakeside Campus, correct, sir?

A: Yes.

Q: You would deny ever yelling or screaming or arguing with staff at the Lakeside Campus?

A: Yes.

Q: And you always conduct yourself in a calm, professional fashion towards your coworkers at the Lakeside Campus, correct, sir?

A: Yes.

Q: You were hospitalized in January of 1995 at the Mendota Mental Health Institute in Madison, correct, sir?

A: Yes, I believe I was.

Q: Are you aware that you were diagnosed as having a passive/aggressive personality disorder and a narcissistic personality disorder, correct, Doctor?

A: That is not correct.

Q: Well, I am taking that right out of the medical records, Dr. White, and you are telling me that you don't have a passive/aggressive personality disorder and a narcissistic personality disorder, correct, Doctor?

A: I believe that the psychiatrist who wrote that report was deposed and explained what he wrote – and I think that was the end of the story.

Q: Well, the criteria for passive/aggressive personality disorder are "Resists fulfilling routine social and occupational tasks, complains of being misunderstood and unappreciated by others, is sullen and argumentative, unreasonably criticizes and scorns authority, expresses envy and resentment towards those apparently more fortunate, voices exaggerated and persistent complaints of personal misfortune, alternates between hostile defiance and contrition." Now, do you believe that those traits identified as accompanying someone with a passive/aggressive personality disorder, that they do not apply to you and how you interact with people at the Lakeside Campus?

A: What you read – it does not apply to me. I am not an expert on psychology, so I don't know the literature you are reading from. All I can tell you is that this is not a description of my behavior in any shape or form. I have worked at a number of institutions and I have interacted with a large number of people without ever demonstrating those characteristics.

Q: Now, here is the description of narcissistic personality disorder: "A pervasive pattern of grandiosity, need for admiration and lack of empathy indicated by five or more of the following: grandiose sense of self importance, preoccupied with fantasies of unlimited success, power, brains, beauty or ideal love, believes he is special and unique and can only be understood by or should associate with other special or high status people or institutions, requires excessive admiration, has a sense of entitlement, i.e., unreasonable expectations of especially favorable treatment or automatic compliance with his or her expectations, is interpersonally exploitative, takes advantage of others to achieve his or her own ends, lacks empathy, is envious of others or believes others are envious of him, shows arrogant, haughty behaviors or attitudes." You don't believe that any of those traits describe the manner in which you conduct yourself, correct, Doctor?

A: I do not believe any of those character traits apply to me. I have always treated my colleagues and the people around me with courtesy and politeness, and my expectations are very limited. I do not envy anybody. I was raised to believe that modesty is a virtue.

Q: Do you have any explanation, then, why your treating psychiatrist assessed you as having a passive/aggressive personality disorder and a narcissistic personality disorder; do you have any idea why he did that?

A: I don't know. And I think he backed off from that assessment in his deposition, and satisfied you that that is not a description of me by any standard.

Q: Did you tell Mary Gregory, the Campus Dean, that you were the only good teacher in the Math Department at Lakeside, and that everybody else who teaches math is terrible?

A: I did not.

Q: Do you believe you are the only competent math teacher at the campus?

A: No, there are others who are very capable.

Q: Haven't you repeatedly criticized the other math teachers on the campus?

A: No, I have not.

Q: So, you would deny ever criticizing the abilities and competence of your fellow instructors of math at the campus?

A: That is correct.

Q: Dr. White, Exhibit 24 is your faculty activity report for the year 1997. In the final section which talks about attainment of goals, you write, "I spent considerable time and effort teaching underprepared students in calculus classes with inflated grades and poor preparation in prerequisite courses." Now, tell me who were the members of the math faculty at Lakeside who gave inflated grades and poorly prepared the students? Whom are you criticizing here?

A: I am not criticizing any particular person, Mr. Fredericks. There are a number of temporary full-time and part-time faculty we hire to teach our math courses. Some of them are not even… don't have a degree in mathematics, and there are discrepancies, and we have tried to make the administration aware of some of these discrepancies repeatedly year after year.

Q: So, you are not criticizing anyone with that comment?

A: It is not for me to criticize any particular person. I was stating a fact.

Q: Is there any chance that the problems within the math department are caused by your inability to get along with your colleagues, John Phillips, Mike Fleck and Ivan Romanov?

A: I get along with everybody just fine.

Q: OK. That's a good answer. You get along just fine with everybody in the math department.

A: I treat them with respect and with dignity. If they have problems with me, I am not aware of it.

Q: Dr. White, I want to read to you an e-mail dated December 5, 1996. It is from Mike Fleck and addressed to Paul Steinman. Fleck writes, "I showed Pete and John what you sent me by campus mail. For my pains, I received a polite 'fine' from John (which is par for the course, John being the gentleman we know), and a stream of non-collegial near shouting from Pete White (which is also par for the course), a response that I now categorize as verbal abuse, and which I told Pete was verbal abuse. I think you need to take matters into your own hands. White tries to twist everything

to make me into either a hatchet man, an unwanted
messenger boy, an incompetent coordinator, sellout,
etc." Now, if you treat Dr. Fleck with collegiality and
professionalism, why would Dr. Fleck write an e-mail
like that to Paul Steinman, saying you verbally abused
him? Why?

A: You have to ask him that question. Mike is quite a
writer. He is responsible for what he writes.

At three o'clock, I set off back to Stanton Hall for my monthly standing meeting with Bob Delaney, chair of the English Department. I met with each of my department chairs once a month, and had quickly decided that there were many advantages to my going to see them in their offices. They liked it because it made them look important to their secretaries and faculty colleagues that the Dean was willing to take the time to go seek them out. I liked it because it got me out of the office and gave me some minimal exercise walking around campus; and at the same time it gave me some visibility on campus with the opportunity to chat with other faculty and secretaries as I walked through the department. It also made it much easier to control the end of the meeting. All I had to do was stand up and say good-bye as I headed for the door. That was harder to do when entertaining a visiting chair in my own office.

Delaney, as an old-timer, had been appropriately skeptical of the new Dean – me – when I first arrived on campus. But he came to understand quickly that my main interest in supervising his work as chair was to help him achieve his and his department's goals. It was an excellent department, they knew what they were doing, they managed their resources frugally, they worked very hard.

Bob and I quickly disposed of the few business issues we had to discuss. I reported that I had approved all of his recommendations for reappointment, and that I had assurance from the Provost that she would also approve them. He announced that he expected Jack Reynolds to announce his retirement within the next few weeks. I urged him to try gently to make that happen as soon as possible. I had no interest – and neither did he – in pushing Reynolds into retirement. But, if we could get an official resignation before Christmas, a replacement search would certainly be authorized. He was grateful for that reassurance.

I asked him how his classes were going. He told me that that evening in his senior seminar world literature class, they were going to be discussing *Crime and Punishment.* I at first felt a little queasy when he said that, but then said to myself, "What the hell, let's talk about *Crime and Punishment.*" I told him that I had first read the novel as a junior in high school, and that my ability to discuss it maturely with my Columbia admissions interviewer had certainly been a positive factor in my eventual acceptance at Columbia.

I told Delaney that I specifically remembered that the interviewer had asked if I identified with Raskolnikov. I had been a little troubled by the question, because as a seventeen year-old I was not really certain about the notion of "identifying with." I told him that the scenes that had really gripped me were the interrogations by the prosecuting attorney who had begun to suspect Raskolnikov. I remembered telling the interviewer that while I could not identify with the decision to kill the old pawnbroker, I did not want Raskolnikov to be caught, and found myself inside his head as he tried to defend himself against the prosecutor's clever questioning.

Bob was interested in my thoughts on the novel since he knew that Russian literature, along with French and English, had been one of my PhD concentrations. We talked about possible ways of approaching the novel with his students. I suggested that he might want to encourage them to debate formally Raskolnikov's theory of the superior human being, who by virtue of his superiority is entitled to transgress ordinary moral codes and social expectations. I also suggested that in some future iteration of the course he might want to include André Gide's novel, *The Vatican Caves*. In fact, I joked that he could create a world literature course with the title "Sympathetic Murderers" or something like that, and also throw in Camus' *The Stranger*. Bob was of course familiar with *The Stranger*, but didn't know the Gide novel. I explained briefly the fascination of the novel's protagonist, Lafcadio, with his innate sense of total freedom which allowed him to decide the fate of another, seemingly insignificant being he encountered in a railroad car, as well as the novel's development of the theory of the "gratuitous act," the motiveless crime. I also reminded him of the character in Balzac's *Père Goriot*, who, when asked how he would respond if he could be assured of a fortune and impunity merely by assenting to the death of an unknown person on the other side of the planet, responded that he was already well beyond his thousandth victim. I later wished I hadn't said all of that...

Continuation of the Deposition of Peter White, PhD
October 3, 1998, 9:04 a.m.

Q: You filed a lawsuit, Dr. White, claiming that you have been discriminated against because of your age and religion with regard to your class teaching schedules at the Lakeside Campus, correct, sir?

A: Yes.

Q: From the fall of 1995 to the present, have you ever been assigned a class teaching schedule that, in your view, was fair and non-discriminatory?

A: Well, I have taught a large number of classes over that span, and I don't remember exactly what in each semester…

Q: Of the last six semesters, were any OK, that is fair and non-discriminatory?

A: I do not remember.

Q: Don't you remember why you filed this lawsuit?

Mr. Cameron: Objection. Argumentative.

Mr. Fredericks: I'll withdraw it.

Q: Let's try it this way. You feel that a two-day a week teaching schedule for yourself is a proper teaching schedule. Isn't that a fair statement?

A: No.

Q: Well, what is a fair teaching schedule for you? What does it have to be to be fair, non-discriminatory, and appropriate for you?

A: Well, the recommendation of the math group on the campus is that courses should be taught in extended sessions of at least eighty minutes. Another recommendation is that faculty have days off to conduct research. And then, classes should preferably not be held very early in the morning, nor late in the evening, and certainly there should be no late night classes followed by an early morning class the next day. And there should not be a long gap during the day between classes

Q: Is it your testimony that if your teaching schedule does not include extended sessions, and days off, has gaps in the scheduling, or has an evening class followed by a morning class, then those factors have been put into your schedule because of your age or religion; is that your testimony?

A: I cannot attest to the motivation, but I know that my peers have not been subjected to the same treatment.

Q: Is it your testimony, then, that if you don't get your preference and what you want, then it's discriminatory?

A: If it is a reasonable request that has proved successful over the years.

Q: Doctor, as I look over the campus teaching schedules for the five semesters starting in the fall of 1996, during these five consecutive semesters, you had a two day a week teaching schedule with Mondays, Wednesdays, and Fridays free, correct?

A: It appears that way.

Q: And in none of those semesters did you have an evening class followed by a class the next morning, right?

A: Correct.

Q: OK, that addresses two out of the four issues you raised. Let's look for extended sessions… In the spring of 1997, you had two sections of Math 141, both taught in extended sessions, correct.

A: Yes.

Q: And it appears to be the case in every one of these semesters that your courses are taught in extended sessions, correct?

A: Yes, but here in the spring of 1998, one course was early in the morning, and the other late in the afternoon.

Q: I see, so there is a concern over the gap you have there, which was one of the four factors. So is the gap in your schedule in that semester discriminatory?

A: Another concern is in the fall of 1997, my classes were scheduled from one to five in the afternoon, back to back, practically without a break.

Q: But it wasn't early morning following a late night, so both courses were in the middle of the day, and now you are complaining about that?

A: It is not in the middle of the day, sir. Both of them are in the afternoon, back to back, from one to five.

Q: Dr. White, have you ever heard Dr. Steinman make any direct comments to you that you viewed as evidencing discrimination on his part towards you because of your age? Has he ever said anything to you that led you to believe it was direct evidence that he was discriminating against you based on your age?

A: Do I remember a word or phrase? No, I do not.

Q: How about with regard to your religion? You are a Mormon, are you not?

A: Yes.

Q: Did he ever say anything to you that you took as being a direct discriminatory statement based on your religion?

A: Several times. He made a comment about an administrator he had known on another campus who was a Mormon, and that the fact she did not drink alcohol was sometimes awkward in social situations. Once he questioned me about the Mountain Meadows Massacre. And then he mentioned on another occasion that he had many years earlier interviewed a candidate for a position teaching French. And he told me he found it strange that that man had greatly improved his ability to speak French by spending two years as a Mormon missionary in France.

Q: Did he explain why he found that strange?

A: Yes, he said that he imagined that it must have been almost impossible to convince the French to give up wine to convert to the Mormon religion.

Q: Did Dr. Steinman say anything else discriminatory?

A: He once boasted to me that he had read the Book of Mormon. He said that when he was in college, he had been approached by missionaries, that he had talked with them at length, and had accepted and then read the Book of Mormon which they gave him. And then he told me, and I found this quite shocking, that he couldn't possibly believe what he had read in the Book of Mormon. And he made a joke about it.

Q: What was the joke?

A: He laughed at the fact that he couldn't believe what was written in the Book of Mormon.

Q: Did you at the time complain about these comments by Dr. Steinman?

A: I did not complain to anyone.

Q: I know you are very familiar with the Affirmative Action Office at the University of Wisconsin. You have filed complaints there before. But you didn't pick up the phone or send a letter to Affirmative Action to complain about these comments by Dr. Steinman?

A: I did not.

Q: Did you send him an e-mail documenting what he had said and telling him how inappropriate it was?

A: No. He was often very insensitive, and I just learned to accept him being that way.

Q: Can you tell me on how many occasions Dr. Steinman made comments that you viewed as discriminatory?

A: I believe he has on a great number of occasions made comments and acted towards me in a discriminatory fashion based on who I am.

Q: You gave examples just now of comments he made about Mormons and the Mormon religion. Please tell me about any other occasions.

A: One occasion which I remember was when he sent me an e-mail and called me, accusing me of insulting a faculty member or something to that effect. I was shocked to hear this accusation, and the tone of his voice was very offensive to me. I checked with people present on the occasion to see if maybe I missed something. I also checked with the students who were present. Nothing happened to cause such an accusation and offensive insult to me.

Q: Was there anything in the e-mail he sent to you on this occasion which referenced your religion or age?

A: Did he specifically say it was because of my religion or my age, no.

Q: You didn't like the tone of his e-mail?

A: I don't think anybody would have liked the tone of that e-mail, Mr. Fredericks.

Q: Do you remember that on this occasion, a faculty member showed up with her class, and that you and your students were already in the classroom assigned to this faculty member?

A: So, you know the occasion. Yes, I was in the classroom with my students.

Q: And it wasn't where your class was assigned to meet at that particular time?

A: When she said that the room was reserved for her and her students, we left the room, and went and found another room.

Q: If that other faculty member wrote a memo saying that you berated and abused her, then you would say that that faculty member is lying, because you conducted yourself appropriately and didn't do anything wrong, is that correct?

A: That is correct.

As I left Delaney's office and headed over to the Theatre Building for my four o'clock standing with Bob Ogleby, chair of Theatre, I promised myself that I would avoid at all cost any discussion of murderers. Even if Ogleby insisted on engaging me in conversations about *Macbeth*, *Hamlet*, or *Richard III* (really unlikely), I would move the conversation towards secondary characters or subtleties of staging, and steer clear of the motivations and self-incriminating errors of Claudius, Macbeth and Richard. Otherwise, I would be haunted by the possibility of an encounter between Ogleby and Delaney in which they might both reflect on the strangely dark preoccupations of the usually cheerful Dean that day.

As it turned out, I needn't have worried. Ogleby was more than a bit rushed. He had a five o'clock rehearsal for the play he was directing, *Three Sisters*, and just wanted to know how his reappointments were going, whether I could support a promotion recommendation for his costumer which his Personnel Committee was considering, and if the college adjunct budget could possibly contribute $5,000 towards the funding of a visiting artist the following fall. I gave him positive answers to all of his concerns, we exchanged some pleasantries, I asked him how his show was going (he was very enthusiastic about it) and I left him at four-thirty.

I went back to my office, answered a couple of routine e-mails, leaving a couple of complicated ones for the next day, returned one call, and then waited patiently in my office until I had heard all of the secretaries on the floor leave promptly at five. Then a few minutes later, I heard Associate Dean Dave Thomas wish me a cheery good evening as he left his office next to mine. Finally, at ten minutes past five, I packed up my briefcase, closed the door behind me and headed for the elevator. I was the last person on the floor to leave, but on the way down, the elevator stopped at the seventh and fifth floors for a few of my administrative colleagues. With one of them, Karen in accounting, I exchanged a smile and greeting. She asked me if I had a relaxed evening planned, and I told her that I was taking home some folders, and hoped to get ahead on my reappointment recommendations, but that I would be watching some Monday night football too.

I left the building and walked to my car at a slow thoughtful pace, so that anyone who noticed might later say, "No, Paul didn't seem to be in any hurry that evening. On the contrary, he was walking slowly, and seemed… thoughtful." It was five twenty-six when I turned on the ignition of my car, and I was at the traffic light at the campus entrance, at exactly five thirty, as I had planned.

Q: Now, I want to be clear on every individual you claim has discriminated against you at the University of Wisconsin from 1995 to the present, and when I say discriminated, I mean harassed you because of complaints you have filed, or discriminated against you because of your age or religion. Can you please identify for me anyone else who has harassed you or discriminated against you?

A: Marjorie Atwood.

Q: And what is her position?

A: She was head of the advising office and worked closely with the Associate Dean. She got students together and passed to them information about me, and encouraged them to complain about me. On one occasion, she apparently invited students for pizza, and then specifically asked them to complain about me. She has been propagating rumors about what I have said or what I have done.

Q: What rumors?

A: Spreading incorrect information about me. I have been told by a number of students negative comments she has made about me, like advising them not to take my classes or not taking me as their advisor. It has been on more than one occasion.

Q: All right. Anything else with her?

A: I cannot remember right now. But, as I said, she was close to the Associate Dean, so my problems with scheduling or teaching or advising students, she was involved in those incidents.

Q: Who else?

A: Jack Burke.

Q: Who is he?

A: He is a member of the faculty and very close to Dr. Gregory, the Campus Dean.

Q: What do you mean by "very close"?

A: He is on every committee. I would say he is the right hand man of Dr. Gregory.

Q: And how has he harassed, discriminated or retaliated against you?

A: In front of others, in a committee meeting, he insulted me.

Q: What did he say?

A: One of the things he said was, "I am sick and tired of disruptions and pissing contests from White." And I wasn't even saying anything. I was shocked.

Q: So, he insulted you by saying he was tired of White's pissing contests. Is that basically what it was?

A: Yes.

Q: Anything else that Mr. Burke, the Dean's right hand man, has done against you. He said he was tired of getting in a pissing contest with you. What else?

A: When a new dean from Madison came to our campus, she had a meeting with the faculty and staff of the campus. I asked a question about program reviews. She said she didn't have the information I requested but said she would find out and get back to me. And then immediately after my question, Mr. Burke asks, "If we have a faculty member who is disruptive and insubordinate, how can you help us get rid of that faculty member." And he asked that question in front of everyone, in front of janitors, in front of maintenance people.

Q: Now, you have also claimed that you were discriminated against in hiring, that you were not offered a position at another University of Wisconsin campus as a result of discrimination on the basis of religion or age. You have specifically mentioned a position at the Parkside Campus.

A: That is correct. I met both the Dean and Associate Dean of the Parkside Campus at a meeting, and they informed me that they had two openings in math that they had been unable to fill in the previous year. I then visited

the campus and met with the head of the math faculty
there. He told me that the positions had been open
for two years, and I told him I would be interested
in transferring to the Parkside Campus because of the
discrimination I faced at Lakeside.

Q: I see no written record of a document, e-mail, letter,
or memo, in which you wrote, "I want to transfer to the
open position at Parkside." Did I miss something?

A: I can't remember. I may have, but usually this is done
verbally, you discuss it with the people involved. And
then there is an agreement between the two campuses.
A number of people have transferred from one place to
another by that procedure,

Q: So, you are saying that you should have received
a position at Parkside, and if you didn't, it was
discriminatory?

A: I believe I could have served them. As the position was
vacant, it would have served all parties, and I think
it would have been a reasonable solution. I believe
it was very odd. I told them I was prepared to accept
the sacrifice of relocating, in order to escape the
hostility I faced at Lakeside. It is true that it would
have benefitted me also, as I was involved in research
that I could have pursued more easily, thanks to the
proximity to Chicago. Anyway, I was very surprised that
initially everything seemed fine, and then as soon as
they started talking to people at Lakeside and found
out more about me, I was denied the transfer, without
any explanation. And I think this is not normal.

Q: But was it discriminatory? Was it because of your age
or religion?

A: I believe so.

Q: Now, Dr. White, you have referred to the research you
were doing in Chicago as the reason you wanted teaching
schedules that left you free on Mondays and Fridays,
and also the reason you wanted to transfer to the
Parkside campus. Were there any personal reasons why
you wanted to spend time in the Chicago area?

A: I have many friends in Chicago. It's a cosmopolitan

city, a very nice city, and I really like Chicago. There are organizations and universities…

Q: Was there any particular person that you wanted to be able to spend time with on a personal basis in the Chicago area that was part of your reason for wanting to do research there?

A: Not initially, no.

Q: Okay, so not initially. But after initially, was there one person in particular with whom you had a personal relationship that you wanted to spend time with? Yes or no.

A: As I said, I have many acquaintances and friends there, perhaps more than any other area…

Q: Dr. White, was there one person in particular, just try and answer my question. Did you have a personal relationship with a female in the Chicago area? There is nothing wrong with that. I just want to know. Did you have a personal relationship with a female in the Chicago area that, at least in part, was behind your desire to want to spend time there, beside the research activities?

Mr. Cameron: Do you really believe that that is related to this case, and do you want him to answer over any objection that I would have?

Mr. Fredericks: Well, he's claiming that one significant part of his case has to do with the way he was treated with regard to what he claimed were research activities that he wanted to be able to do in the Chicago area. He claims that's why he wanted Mondays and Fridays off from teaching, and why he wanted to transfer to the Parkside Campus. He claims that he was treated unfairly with regard to his teaching schedule over an extended period of time, and unfairly denied a transfer to the Parkside Campus.

I'm exploring the issue because we don't believe there's any documentation that any research activities were going on, and I am asking if there is some other reason – and I am permitted to explore this – that explains why he wanted to be near Chicago. That's the explanation.

Mr. Cameron: OK, he can go ahead and answer it.

Q: When did your personal relationship with whoever it is in the Chicago area begin?

A: It was about three years ago.

Q: Is this part of the reason why you would like to teach at a location such as the Parkside Campus, for example, which would be closer to Chicago?

A: Geographic proximity was definitely a factor, but first of all I wanted to be on another campus where I would not be continually harassed. I was ready to leave the home in which I was living, and go through hardship just to get away from the Lakeside Campus and the administrators there who were causing me so much trouble.

I got off the Thruway at my Saint Paul exit, as I did every evening, filled the car with gas at the Exxon Station, and paid cash. I got back on I-94 east and headed towards Wisconsin. It was just past six-thirty when I got to the bridge at Hudson. The trip from there to Lakeside would take a good four hours, so I was right on schedule. White, who lived alone since his wife had left him, didn't go to bed until midnight, and he came down to the kitchen at about eleven-thirty every evening to pour himself a glass of milk.

How did I know that? Well, he had told me so himself, years earlier when our relations were somewhat cordial, and we had a discussion about anxiety and sleeping difficulties. And I had verified it myself five months earlier, when I was still living in the area, and this middle of the night project was just beginning to form in my mind. In late June, during my last week working at the Lakeside Campus, I had spent two long evenings at the office ("lot of stuff to finish up and files to straighten out before I leave" in case I encountered anyone there, but I didn't), and took advantage of those opportunities to check out the parking lot of the nearby Forest Grove apartment complex, where I thought I could park my car unnoticed, and from which I could walk about five minutes through the woods to the clearing which offered an unobstructed view of Pete White's refrigerator through the kitchen window. On the nights of June 24 and 25, I had stood on the edge of that clearing, crouched behind a tree, pointing an imaginary rifle towards the window of White's kitchen. On the first night, at eleven twenty-six, and on the second night at eleven twenty-eight, White, clad in his pajamas, had been clearly visible in the window, opening the refrigerator. The guy was clockwork.

Continuation of the Deposition of Peter White, PhD
October 3, 1998, 9:04 a.m.

Q: Dr. White, your classes are routinely evaluated using the math department evaluation forms, are they not?

A: Yes.

Q: Now when using these forms for evaluation, do you remain present in the class when the forms are distributed to the students and filled out by them?

A: No.

Q: You've never done that?

A: No.

Q: It is your testimony under oath that you have never personally distributed or collected the math department teaching evaluation forms?

A: Yes.

Q: And is it your testimony under oath that you have never been present in the classroom while the students were completing the math department student evaluation forms?

A: To my recollection, yes, that is usually the practice. We leave the room.

Q: I'm not asking usually, Doctor. I want to know...

A: That is exactly what I do.

Q: And if students were to testify that you have been present to either pass out, collect or be there while the forms were completed, they would be incorrect in those statements, correct?

A: Yes.

Q: Dr. White, I am going to show you what I have marked as Exhibit 47. This is a copy of an article that you produced to me through your attorney in the course of this litigation, correct, sir?

A: Yes.

Q: Now, the article that you produced in discovery which was in response to a request for all documents that support any of the claims you made in your faculty activity report, entitled, "Application of Dynamic Neural Networks to Approximation and Control of Nonlinear Systems," shows yourself, P. White, as the sole and exclusive author of the article, correct, sir?

A: Can you restate your question?

Q: You have a doctorate, and are a full professor at the University of Wisconsin, but you don't understand the question I just asked you; is that your testimony?

Mr. Cameron: Note my objection to the form of the question.

Mr. Fredericks: Withdraw.

Q: Doctor, very simply, Exhibit 47, did you write that article?

A: Yes, this is a paper which I started with some other colleagues, and which I submitted through my attorney along with other preprints and papers which I had in my office.

Q: Dr. White, did you write the article labeled Exhibit 47 upon which you put your name only as the author. Did you write it yourself?

A: I answered you.

Q: Did you write the article? Yes or no? That's a simple question. Did you write the article?

A: This was an article...

Q: Doctor, did you write the article? Then you may explain. Yes or no?

A: I believe so. I don't know what you mean by writing. Did I write by handwriting it? Or are you saying did I prepare this paper? I do not understand your...

Q: Doctor, on Exhibit 47, you identify yourself as the only author of that article, correct? Yes or no?

A: Yes.

Q: And in academics that means something, correct? You are identifying yourself as the individual who conceived of and wrote that article, correct, sir?

A: Not necessarily. First of all, when you do a joint paper with someone, and later there is a modification to the paper and the other authors are not interested in the article, you would do that. If you are writing a preprint on a subject on which you have done research with others, and then submit it to a conference, and the others are not interested, you may submit it... I don't understand what you are implying.

Q: I am not implying.

A: It is very clear that this is a preprint, a paper, and my name is on it...

Q: Doctor, is it your testimony under oath that you did not plagiarize the article labeled Exhibit 47?

Mr. Cameron: Please note my objection. This appears to be outside the parameters of the lawsuit. May I have a moment with my client?

Mr. Fredericks: No, I don't think it's appropriate for you to take time with your client when there's a question like that pending.

Mr. Cameron: Well, then, I'll just have him refuse to answer. It's not part of this lawsuit, it doesn't appear. You're going on a fishing expedition into any type of alleged misconduct...

Mr. Fredericks: Counsel, for the record, his claim is that he has been treated unfairly with regard to his salary beginning in 1995. Salary calculations are based on the faculty activity report as submitted. I am entitled to explore with this gentleman whether, in fact, he has done everything he says he has done on the faculty activity reports he submitted.

Mr. Cameron: Go ahead, ask your question.

Q: The question, as I recall, was very simple. Did you

plagiarize this article from someone else, this article being Exhibit 47? Yes or no?

A: No.

Q: Well, Doctor, I have a copy of an article entitled, , "Application of Dynamic Neural Networks to Approximation and Control of Nonlinear Systems," published by Drs. Avery, Reinhart and Wang, in the proceedings of the American Control Conference, Tucson, Arizona, June 1994, pages 222 through 226. I have compared the article to what you have identified here as an article of the same title with your name only listed as author, and I will tell you that I find it basically word-for-word the same as the article you claim as your work.

So, let me ask you again, did you copy the article labeled Exhibit 47 from an article written by Drs. Avery, Reinhart and Wang bearing the same title? Yes or no?

A: No.

Q: In 1996, in your faculty activity report, you claim you presented a paper at the fourth ICIAM conference in Edinburgh, Scotland. Do you recall making that claim?

A: I do not recall that. Can I have a look to see what I have written…?

Q: Well, do you recall going to a conference in Edinburgh, Scotland, in 1995?

A: Yes.

Q: OK, good. Now, on your faculty activity report for that year, under the section reserved for papers presented at professional meetings, you list a paper presented at the Fourth International Congress on Industrial and Allied Mathematics, in Edinburgh, Scotland, in July 1995, and have included the words "invited paper" in parentheses. Now, I have gone to the speakers' index for that conference, and your name does not appear on it. Can you explain that to me, Dr. White?

A: Yes, first of all the names of all of the presenters

do not appear in the index. In conferences as large as this one, there are a number of sessions and presentations which crop up. On a number of occasions I have attended conferences during which I have been asked spontaneously to give a talk on the subject of my current research. I had not previously submitted this paper to the selection committee for the conference, but made the presentation in response to an ad hoc request. Therefore, my name does not appear in the index.

Q: Doctor, did you present a paper at the Fourth ICIAM Conference in Edinburgh, Scotland, in July of 1995? Yes or no?

A: I presented my research in response to an invitation from people attending that conference.

Q: Did you present the paper at the meeting, yes or no?

A: Depends on what you mean by presentation. Yes, I did give a lecture about my paper. I was asked to present my research and I did. Did I submit a paper to the conference organizing committee? No, I did not.

Q: Who asked you to do the presentation?

A: There were a number of people interested.

Q: Who? Give me their names.

A: I do not recall right now the names.

Q: What was the topic of the particular break-out session in which you presented this paper?

A: If I had the program of the conference in front of me, I could identify the particular session.

Q: How long did it take for you to present your paper?

A: I don't know.

Q: Do you have any proof that you made this presentation? No speakers' index, no copy of the article, no letters from anyone present, you don't have anything you can show me, right?

A: I do not have any documents right now. But yes, I made the presentation, in the sense that if you discuss your interests and give a presentation to a few people in a conference, that is according to my criteria a presentation at a professional conference. If that doesn't meet your criteria, I am sorry.

By seven p.m., I was on the quiet stretch of I-94 around Menomonie. It was at a gun show in Menomonie that I had bought my M-1 Carbine three months earlier. If you want to buy a gun at a licensed gun show, you have to fill out federal forms. But there is a gun selling subculture which has developed in the parking lots around arenas where the official shows are held. There, buyers and sellers come to terms, and exchange weapons for cash with no questions asked, and practically no paperwork at all. I gave a guy named Hank $525 and a fake name and address for his receipt, and he handed me an M-1 Carbine from the trunk of his car. As simple as that. I had modified my dress and grooming to be as unmemorable as possible that day, in case someday, some police agent traced the gun to that seller. On-line research had convinced me that the M-1 Carbine was the gun for me. It had the range, accuracy, and ease of operation I needed, and they were relatively inexpensive (I had seen them available on-line in the $500 range). Cost was important because I planned to pay with cash, and I didn't want to have made any suspiciously large cash withdrawals in the time leading up to the purchase. Since the 1940s, more than five million M-1 Carbines have been produced, and they are easily available at gun shows. And in the parking lot outside.

Learning to use it accurately had required some planning and serious work. I hadn't shot anything but my son's BB gun since the time when I was a teen and my cousin Syd had taken me hunting with his .22 in the woods behind his parents' house. I considered briefly enrolling in an NRA safety course, but decided that was too visible; someone might remember the balding, plump professor. For similar reasons I had to reject asking one of my hunting friends for help. ("Yes, matter of fact, I was surprised when Paul, who had never shown any interest in hunting, suddenly wanted to learn to shoot.") It was obvious I had to teach myself. I bought a manual at a second hand bookstore, read it carefully, then one day after work, took the rifle to a remote wooded area next to Lake Winnebago (that required some scouting), and practiced for an hour shooting at a target. (I knew that if I was discovered, it would jeopardize the project, but if what I was doing was illegal and I was caught, I reasoned that the consequences would be minimal.) It wasn't really hard after a while to hit a target, especially while supporting the rifle in the notch of a tree.

I was still feeling a little insecure about my shooting ability, when, about a month later, I got lucky. Right after moving to the Saint Paul area, I had joined a small tennis club. I had quickly discovered that one of the club's members, a good tennis player named Pete Atherton, was also an avid hunter and sport shooter. He talked about it a lot, but I showed little interest. (No way he could later tell someone, "Yes, that is true, every time I talked about hunting and shooting, Paul always wanted to know more.") But then one day in September, Pete sent around an e-mail notice that at the club sponsored steak barbecue at the Farrell's lakeside cottage, he would bring his rifles and skeets, and anyone interested could learn how to shoot. I had already responded that I would be at the barbecue, and I figured that most of those attending the barbecue would take part in Pete's shooting seminar.

When I showed up, I feigned total ignorance and only mild interest in the shooting event. I listened carefully to his advice about hand placement, the position of the rifle butt against my shoulder (which varied a bit from the manual I had read), and the use of the sight. I intentionally missed the first three skeets I shot at pretty badly. But then, on the fourth, I did everything exactly right, and hit the skeet very squarely. We laughed about that. I said, "Hey, this is easy!" And of course the onlookers yelled back, "Beginner's luck." I then intentionally missed the next four to confirm that my square hit had been a fluke. Thanks to Pete, I had learned a little more about how to shoot. But, more importantly, the opportunity to shoot successfully at a moving target, with someone else's rifle, and without a brace, had given me a lot of confidence. And I had also created the impression among a pretty good sized crowd of people that I was a hapless professor with no sense of how to fire a rifle.

I had thought about trying to find and use another rifle that would be impossible to trace to me. But all of the plans I imagined seemed too complicated and dangerous. The better – but still far from perfect – plan was to use my M-1, be certain that no one ever found out I had it, and to bury it where it was extremely unlikely that anyone would find it. There would remain the unlikely but possible scenario that someday, someone would come upon the buried rifle, turn it over to the police who would identify it as the murder weapon, and trace it to the gun dealer from Menomonie. If that dealer happened to have a remarkably strong enough recall of faces to pick me out of a lineup as the purchaser of his rifle, then, and only then, would I have to call upon a good lawyer, and everything else I had done to cover up my traces, to protect myself from a murder conviction. As I said, not a perfect plan, but a very good one, I thought.

After exiting from I-94 onto Route 29 at Eau Claire, I went through in my mind everything else I needed to do to cover up my tracks. Was there any chance that someone would notice my Subaru Legacy in the parking lot of the Forest Grove apartments in Lakeside? Not really. There were lots of Subaru Legacies in the area. I still had my Wisconsin plates. I had removed my hanging USP parking sticker, which might have attracted attention. The two nights in June when I had parked there, I had not seen another car come out of or go into the lot during the hour I was parked there.

I would surely leave some kind of footprints at the edge of the clearing from which I had the view into White's kitchen, and those footprints might be traceable from the clearing to the parking lot. I was wearing a very ordinary pair of old dress shoes, that I hadn't worn in years and that I planned to dispose of on the ride home (along with the spent shells hidden in a cigarette pack). But I had no plan to try to obliterate completely my path from the parking lot to the clearing and then back. Would my car leave any traceable tire tracks? I wasn't really sure. All of the roads I was traveling were very dry. I couldn't imagine I would leave identifiable tracks in the apartment lot, even if some smart police detective figured out that that is where the murderer had parked. I was relatively comfortable that neither tire tracks nor foot prints would be traceable to me. And I would wear light gloves to eliminate any finger prints.

The big question of course was whether or not I would be suspected. If so, they would certainly want to search my house for a gun that matched the bullets and shoes that matched the footprints in the woods. They would find neither. On the odd chance that I had left a tire track, they would be able to verify that my very common Bridgestones did match the track. But that, I imagined, would be very slim evidence.

From the Deposition of Anthony Russo, PhD
September 4, 1998, 8:37 a.m.

Q: Dr. Russo, as you know, my name is Elliot Cameron. I represent Peter White in a case brought against the University of Wisconsin. I have asked you to come here today to answer some questions about matters relating to the case. If I ask you anything that is not clear, that you don't understand, please tell me. Dr. Russo, by whom are you employed?

A: The University of Wisconsin

Q: How long have you been at the University of Wisconsin?

A: I came in the fall of 1989.

Q: What is your academic field?

A: Philosophy.

Q: Am I correct that you were involved with what is known as the STS program?

A: That is correct.

Q: What is the STS program?

A: STS stands for Science, Technology and Society. It is an interdisciplinary program of the university created to promote teaching and research on the relations between science, technology and societal issues.

Q: At some point, am I correct, you became the director of STS?

A: That's correct, I was appointed director by the dean in 1991.

Q: You know Peter White?

A: Yes, I do. I think we first met in the fall of 1992.

Q: Under what circumstances?

A: He came and introduced himself to me. He told me a little bit about his work, that he was from the Lakeside

Campus, and that he was interested in volunteering to do some work with STS.

Q: What reaction did you have?

A: I was always looking for volunteers, and told him that was great.

Q: What do you mean "volunteers?"

A: Faculty take it upon themselves to say that this is something they want to do. It is not part of their required work, but they do need permission of their supervisor.

Q: Do you mean they do it in addition to their required work?

A: That's often the case, yes.

Q: After the initial meeting with Dr. White, did he develop any association with the STS program?

A: Yes, he taught a course, I don't recall exactly when.

Q: After he taught that course, was there any further involvement by Dr. White in the STS program?

A: He became a member of the Executive Committee.

Q: Do you know when?

A: I think that was in the spring of 1993.

Q: In the spring of 1995, did you become aware that Dr. White was dissatisfied with your directorship of the STS program?

A: Yes, but I did not hear that directly from him.

Q: From whom did you hear that?

A: From my colleague Richard Wilson who replaced me as acting director of the program for a semester while I was on leave.

Q: Did Richard Wilson suggest to you in any way that Dr. White was in some way leader of a movement or a group to have you replaced?

A: Yes.

Q: How did you feel about knowing that there was dissatisfaction with you as director?

A: A little unhappy.

Q: Only a little?

A: I think my primary feeling was one of asking myself – a kind of self-examination – was I really doing a good job? What should I do? Should I resign? There was unhappiness too because this created distractions when I was on leave trying to write a book.

Q: Did you feel under some sort of personal attack?

A: Only moderately. I didn't feel like the attack was personal. There was basic disagreement about goals and orientation. I was also sure that the move by White was self-serving, that he was hoping to get himself appointed Director, but I was confident that would never happen.

Q: Did you tell anybody outside of STS, other than your wife and family, that there was dissatisfaction with you within STS?

A: I may have.

Q: Did you tell Paul Steinman about Dr. White's involvement?

A: It is likely that I did.

Q: Why?

A: White works at Lakeside, we both know him, we are sharing our experiences.

Q: Did he say that Dr. White caused dissension at Lakeside?

A: He indicated to me at some time that there had been problems with Dr. White at Lakeside, yes. He told me something about a course that Dr. White didn't want to teach – there was some kind of problem with the facilities, smoke in a building. I remember him saying that there was an issue involved with smoke, and that Dr. White refused to teach.

Q: Did Dr. Steinman say that he wanted Dr. White to teach in a class that had smoke in it?

A: No.

Q: Did you tell Dr. Steinman that you were unhappy about Dr. White being involved in the dissatisfaction with you as director?

A: I don't know.

Q: May have?

A: May have.

At about eight forty-five, an event occurred which dramatically interrupted my travel along Route 29, and which I include with some reluctance in this narrative. I fear it may be perceived as an attempt to arouse sympathy and understanding for me, as I did exhibit in this circumstance character traits that might tend to redeem me. I am not trying to portray myself as a heroic figure; I am not. I am surprised at what I did, and tend to attribute it to an elevated hormonal state which my deadly fixation of the evening had stimulated.

At any rate, as I was driving along Route 29 at about eight-thirty, I found myself behind an oil truck. I followed the truck for approximately fifteen miles. It was moving fast enough so that I felt no real need to pass to maintain my schedule, and besides the road twists and turns a lot between Thorp and Abbotsford, with very few opportunities to pass. It was clearly not in my interest to take any risks that might lead to an accident or police interference, so I patiently stayed behind the truck.

But then I began to notice erratic behavior on the part of the driver. At first barely perceptible swerves became more pronounced and frequent. Then there was a big swerve across the median into the oncoming lane, and I was about to lean on my horn when abruptly the truck straightened its trajectory. For a mile or two it appeared that the driver had regained control of himself and his truck, but I was troubled and wondered if I should intervene. Then, as we entered a long slow curve to the left, before I could fully register what was happening, the truck kept going straight, through the guard rail, and down a slight embankment. I slammed on my brakes, and watched through my rear view mirror as the truck, in what appeared to be slow motion animation, rolled over two or three times before coming to a stop, upside down in a field, about two hundred yards behind where my car stopped safely on the shoulder.

I backed my car to within about fifty feet of the spot where the truck had gone off the road, jumped out of the car, and clambered down the embankment into the field. The scene was eerily quiet; the giant tanker lay on its roof. Suddenly I was aware of a strong odor of gasoline, and heard what must have been hundreds of gallons pouring from the tank. There was smoke coming from the engine, and I knew I had to act quickly. I raced to the cab, saw through the window that the driver was upside down, apparently unconscious, his face bloodied, and still held in place by his seat belts. The cab door was unlocked, and I was able to open it easily. Wedging my back against the driver to release the pressure on the seat belt, I unfastened it, and when I felt his full weight on my back, I crawled backwards out of the cab on to the ground. I turned him on his back, grabbed him under the armpits and backed my way as fast as I could up the embankment onto the highway shoulder; at that moment a flash of light followed by a loud explosion alerted me that the truck had caught fire. I looked down, and saw that the cab was engulfed in flames, as was the field for several dozen yards all around it where the gasoline had spread.

The driver was aroused by the sound of the explosion. He turned to me with a look that eased from panic to a grim ironic smile, as he realized that he was safe.

Within a minute, attracted by the harsh light of the fire which highlighted the two of us on the highway shoulder, one car, then a second slammed to a halt. An elderly couple, then a boy possibly still in his teens emerged from their cars and ran to us as the truck driver was groggily getting to his feet. I saw the older man pull out a cell phone, and with all three of the rescuers turning their backs to me, I walked deliberately the fifty feet to my car, and drove off, before they appeared to notice that I had left them. Through my rear view mirror, the last thing I saw was the three rescuers absorbed in conversation with the truck driver. I continued to drive away from the scene, and within a mile or two, I saw the emergency lights of a state trooper coming quickly in my direction, and knew that more help was on the way.

About forty-five minutes later as I approached Waupaca on Route 54, despite the dramatic interruption in my plans, I still had forty-five minutes to burn sometime between then and my arrival at the Forest Grove parking lot. I wanted to fill the car with gas. I was hungry and knew there was an IHOP at the Northgate Mall that would do the trick: it was far enough away from Lakeside so that the chance of running into someone I knew was very slim, close enough so that I could be very sure of the remaining time to my destination, forty-five minutes. I wanted to be in the parking lot at eleven fifteen, giving myself five minutes to walk to the clearing, and no more than ten minutes to wait for White to appear in the kitchen window.

Before going into the IHOP, I examined my face in the car mirror, and saw no traces of blood or dirt. However, my overcoat had blood stains from the truck driver's face, so I took it off, rolled it up, and threw it into the trunk before going into the restaurant.

I ordered scrambled eggs, toast and pancakes, and ate them slowly while working on the Times Sunday Puzzle from the previous day's Magazine Section, which I had already started. I was surprised to find myself calm and focused, "Former first name in Israeli politics." Golda. "The Big Sleep Costar." Bogart. I chatted politely with the server, but tried to say nothing that would attract notice or cause her to remember me afterwards. I casually looked around at the other customers in the restaurant, a young couple, two middle-aged women, and a few solitary travelers like myself. I wasn't even thinking about White.

I paid cash, left a reasonable tip, and walked out to my car at exactly ten-thirty. As I had calculated, it took me forty-five minutes to drive down Route 10 to the Route 114 exit at Lakeside, and take Route 114 out through town to the Forest Grove Apartments. While driving, I found the Monday night football game, Broncos vs. the Chargers, on ESPN radio, and listened long enough to be able to talk about the game in case someone asked me if I had watched it. I saw no one as I parked in the lot of the Forest Grove Apartments. I took the gun case out of the trunk and walked the three hundred yards through the woods to the Deer Trail Apartments where Peter White lived, and where he would a few minutes later die, while standing by his refrigerator, enjoying a glass of milk.

Continuation of the Deposition of Anthony Russo, PhD
September 4, 1998, 8:37 a.m.

Q: Do you know how it came about that Dr. White stopped having an office in the STS program area?

A: I asked him to vacate his office.

Q: Why?

A: Because he was no longer teaching at Madison, and reallocations of office space needed to be made.

Q: Did Paul Steinman ask you to have Dr. White vacate his office at STS?

A: No, he did not.

Q: Dr. Russo, I want to show you what's marked as Exhibit P-60. Tell me what this is.

A: This is a letter to Dr. White.

Q: From you?

A: From me.

Q: You sent this to him on July 5, 1995.

A: That's correct.

Q: In the first sentence, it says that because he did not vacate his office and was out of town, "I was obliged to box up your books and about half of the materials and place them in the storage room." What is the source of the obligation to which you are referring?

A: Contingencies that I felt I needed to meet. Obliged by circumstances, not by persons.

Q: The next to the last paragraph refers to Dr. White's past behavior, and because of that, you've notified police services to be present when he comes to reclaim his possessions. What past behavior are you talking about?

A: A number of people had felt that he had acted somewhat irrationally with them in their presence.

Q: Were you afraid of Dr. White?

A: Yes, I was.

Q: Based on what?

A: There had been a number of situations reported in newspapers of workplace violence involving people who felt they had been mistreated. My impression was that Dr. White felt he had been treated unfairly. I didn't want to be responsible for not having taken prudent precautions. This was shortly after a faculty member in Montreal had killed two or three professors. I felt like it was prudent. Not that I was thinking that Dr. White is out gunning for me, but you try to be as prudent as possible in situations like this.

Q: People had told you things that led you to conclude that it would be prudent to notify police services, is that right?

A: The general tenor of the relationship, as I interpreted it, between Dr. White and others in the STS program and people at the University, yes, led me to conclude that.

Q: When did you conclude that?

A: When I realized that Dr. White was not going to remove his own things voluntarily, but that I was going to have to take action to get them moved, that's when I concluded that I ought to… I actually contacted somebody in the dean's office about this, and they suggested that I contact police services to get advice on how to do this. I talked to them, and asked if the situation ever came up when faculty members would not vacate offices, and they said, oh yes, and here is what we suggest.

Q: Did they suggest that you have one of the security people be present when he comes for his stuff?

A: Yes, they did.

Q: Did you suggest to them that there was reason for concern?

A: I suggested to them that there was some reason for

concern. I said I was concerned that the situation might escalate and things might get out of control.

Q: What are the facts upon which you drew your conclusions about the general tenor of relationships?

A: Reports from Richard Wilson about White's confrontational attitude in Executive Committee meetings, and my secretary's reports of confrontational episodes with Dr. White in the office are the primary ones.

Q: Your secretary reported confrontation?

A: Yes.

Q: What was the confrontation she reported?

A: She reported that it was difficult for her to deal with White about classes, about access to the office, and about the student he had working for him. And that there was one instance in which she felt threatened by Dr. White in the parking lot.

Q: In the parking lot?

A: Yes.

Q: Did he raise his voice to her, as you understood it?

A: Yes, as she reported it to me.

I was already back on Route 10 by midnight, heading towards Waupaca, listening to the end of the Monday Night Football game. Everything had gone exactly as I had planned. After the shooting I had stood in the clearing for a minute, listening for any reaction to the sound of my gun. There was none. I had to resist the sudden unexpected temptation to drop the rifle there, and spare myself the chore of burying it. I had already weighed the options. Burying it gave me one additional layer of security, as long as no one saw me, and so that was clearly the better course. I would have to be completely sure there were no other cars around when I pulled into Brown Creek State Park outside of Waupaca to bury the rifle. If I left the rifle behind, the police would have the murder weapon, but no clear traceable path to me, unless the gun dealer had a remarkable memory for faces and the police already suspected me. But that was possible. Better to leave the gun somewhere it was unlikely to be found, and fifty miles from the crime.

I felt fine. No regrets, no guilt. I began to wonder how quickly the news would spread. What if one of my former Lakeside colleagues heard the news right away, and then tried to call me, and was subsequently surprised that I was not home? The campus police would probably learn of the murder right away, through monitoring of the police broadcasts, or they might get a direct call. They would certainly notify the Campus Dean, Mary Gregory, even though it was after midnight, and the word would spread quickly. But why would anyone call me? And besides, I could always claim I had gone to sleep and had not heard the home phone ring. And, in fact, why would anyone discover the murder that night? There had been no immediate reaction to the rifle shots. Lying on the kitchen floor, White was not visible from outside the apartment. There were two bullet holes in the window, but who would notice? He lived alone, estranged from his wife and kids. How long might he lay dead before anyone discovered him? He had no Tuesday classes, so it would not be until Wednesday that the campus would begin to be aware that he was missing. There were rain showers forecast for Tuesday night. That might wash away all traces of my passage before anyone even began to suspect that something was wrong.

Actually nothing was wrong, and life at the Lakeside Campus was about to become "right" again. And that was what this was all about. Mostly. The initial motivation for my crime was very simply the altruistic desire to make things right for my former colleagues and the students of the campus. During my seven years as Associate Dean of the campus, I had often thought to myself that it was unfair that the life of the campus, and the lives of the hundreds of people who worked and studied there were tormented – the word is not too strong – by the cruelly selfish and manipulative behavior of a narcissistic maniac. How many times had I wished for an accident that would put an end to his reign of terror? Not so much to spare myself the mayhem and consternation that I had to deal with directly, but mostly for the others. It was my concern for the others that had ultimately got me imagining this solution, the elimination of Peter White, after I had left the campus, when it could in no way benefit me personally, and therefore when I would never be suspected of the crime. Having left the campus, I would immediately benefit from a protective shield around me. I would be off the list of all of the people in the world who might desire the death of Peter White.

While I conceived the project as predominantly altruistic, there was a secondary self-indulgent motivation. I enjoyed imagining myself as a Gidean/Dostoyevskian hero, committing a murder within an intellectual framework. The altruistic motivation, one might argue, distinguishes my act from Gide's "acte gratuit." But since the altruistic motivation includes no personal gain, is it not at least partially gratuitous? An important component of Lafcadio's motivation in Gide's *The Vatican Caves* is that he will not be suspected of the murder because he has no association with the victim and no reason to murder him. I do have an association with my victim, but it is a past association, and any reason for murdering him would seem to have been left behind when I left the campus. Being beyond suspicion had become motivating. I was sure I could get away with it.

I was sure I could get away with it legally. But what about moral responsibility? I was going to take a man's life. Wouldn't that make me an evildoer? And at that point in the discussion with myself I took up Raskolnikov's mantle of moral superiority, and convinced myself that any moral guilt for the taking of White's life was nullified by the man's worthlessness. He would be mourned by some perhaps, missed by his children perhaps. But that would be a good thing for him. Hundreds would secretly, or perhaps even overtly, applaud his death. That a few would be sad and regretful was a destiny to be desired. If his children had not already figured out or been told by their mother that he was a bad person, they would have eventually come to understand that.

His premature death will give him an enhanced stature he could not have earned by himself. "This is for your own good, Pete." All of that might very well have been intellectual self-delusion, I knew, but I didn't care. It made it easier for me to commit an act I was perfectly comfortable committing. And I was pretty certain I would never have to justify it to anyone else.

On Route 10, just west of Waupaca, I exited onto Route 54 which I took to Brown Creek Road. There was a quarter mile stretch of road between the park entrance and the gate and booth where in the summer you paid the entrance fee. Of course the booth would be empty and the gate closed. So I had figured that at one a.m. on a Monday in November, I could pretty safely bury the gun in the woods along the side of the entrance road. It seemed important that no one see me turn off into the park entrance, so I made sure no cars were visible coming either way. If I had seen a car, I was prepared to go beyond the entrance and then stop and turn back. If by some unfortunate chance a police car saw me and followed me, I was prepared to tell them that I desperately needed to relieve myself. There were no cars in sight. I drove about half-way to the gate, stopped the car and waited to make sure no one had followed me. After three minutes, I took the shovel and gun case out of the trunk, quickly dug a hole about two feet deep by the side of the road, buried the case with the gun in it, cleaned off the shovel, covered the spot with leaves, put the shovel in the trunk, and got back in the car. I had seen a couple of cars travel by on Brown Creek Road, but no one had taken any interest in me or my car. I pulled back out onto the road, and sighed audibly. I realized that that had been the part of the whole plan that had stressed me the most: the disposal of the weapon. This was not a perfect solution, I knew, but it was the best one I could come up with, and it had gone according to plan. I could now relax and enjoy the rest of the ride home, not forgetting to dispose of my shoes, my stained overcoat, and the cigarette box with the spent shells in a trash barrel at the highway rest area on I-94.

I pulled into my driveway just after four-fifteen a.m. No lights on, no one visible in the neighborhood. No messages on the phone answering machine. I turned on my home computer to make sure I hadn't missed any important e-mail messages. Nothing. I went to bed and slept soundly until the alarm jarred me awake at seven-thirty. I would be a little late for work, and maybe a little less alert than normal throughout the day, but no one would notice.

PART TWO: Preliminary Investigation

One

The body in fact lay undiscovered until Thursday morning. From what I could tell from reading the Friday *Riverdale Post Tribune* on-line on Friday morning, December 4, Gary Baker, head of campus police, had gone to White's apartment on Thursday, after White had failed to show up for classes on Wednesday and didn't answer phone calls or e-mails. He spotted the broken window and saw the body on the floor. He immediately broke into the apartment and called the local police after determining that White was indeed dead and had been so for some time. Homicides were rare in the area, so the paper gave the story a lot of coverage with enough details about the controversy surrounding White to create an image of a man whose passing some people would not regret. There were flattering comments from students about how he had pushed them to high levels of achievement. The official statement from the Campus Dean Mary Gregory expressed the deep distress of the campus over the loss of an esteemed colleague and eminent mathematician.

I got my first personal notification later that same afternoon, an e-mail from English professor Steve Weston, who wanted to make sure I had heard the dreadful news. His message oozed with undisguised irony and glee. I e-mailed him back later to express my wonderment. I told him that after reading his message, I had gone to the *Post Tribune* website (didn't tell him I had erased the earlier visit to the site from my Internet Explorer History), and found the whole story bizarre and surprising. I concluded my message, "We all disliked him of course, but who would want to kill him?" Later in the course of that weekend, I had e-mails from three other former Lakeside colleagues, who wanted to make sure I knew about it.

It was two weeks later before I heard from the Outagamie County Sheriff's Office. I had been expecting that, and in a peculiar way looking forward to it. From the follow-up newspaper stories, and from information forwarded to me by former colleagues, it was clear that the police had no leads. I was pretty sure that they would want to talk with me. In the week following the murder, Laura Higgins, the University of Wisconsin attorney representing us in the White lawsuit, had called me to say that we no longer needed to get together to rehearse my testimony. I had taken advantage of her call to ask what the police had found as far as clues to the identity of the murderer. She said she hadn't heard much, but she had the feeling they were stumped. In the absence of any real clues, there was some willingness to believe it might have been an accident. The time elapsed between the death and the discovery of the body had left the police without a clear time of death, and so they were willing to believe that he might have been killed by a stray bullet from some deer hunter taking advantage of the opening of the season that Monday. White was wearing pajamas and drinking a glass of milk in the kitchen when he was hit, which suggested that he had been shot while preparing breakfast Monday or Tuesday morning.

I was surprised to discover that the conversation with Laura left me with mixed feelings. On one hand, it was extraordinary good luck that the evening rain on Tuesday had probably washed away my footprints and tire tracks, and that the delay in discovering the body had made it impossible to pinpoint the time of death, so that the police might easily conclude that White's death was the result of a hunting accident. While it got me off the hook, it also got Pete White off the hook, so to speak. It left him as the innocent victim of a tragic freak accident. If people thought he died at the hand of some inept hunter who might be totally unaware of his act, it seemed to me that justice was ill served. I wanted the world to be aware that Pete White had died because of who he was, as the result of a well-executed act of justice. It seemed to me that a careful investigation would have revealed that it was not an accident. I had seen enough TV crime shows to know that an analysis of the bullet impacts on White and the cabinet behind him would surely reveal that the bullet had been fired from a distance of fifty yards from the point in the clearing where I had stood, and that it was not aimed at a deer but through the window at him. I was disappointed that the Outagamie County Sheriff's Office, charged with the investigation, was not going to be a more fearsome adversary. My disappointment, however, was short-lived.

I got the call on Monday, December 21. I was in the office as we wouldn't be officially closing for the holidays until Wednesday evening. The campus was very quiet that day; students had gone home, and faculty were grading final exams to get grades in before the end of the week. At about ten-fifteen, Sue called in to me with a bit of a puzzled sound in her voice that I had a call from the Outagamie County Sheriff's Office. I picked up after waiting fifteen seconds:

"Hello, this is Paul Steinman."

"Dean Steinman, this is Fred Jameson from the Outagamie County Sheriff's Office. I'm a homicide inspector looking into the death of Peter White. I understand that you knew him?"

"Yes, of course I did. I was his dean while I was at the Lakeside Campus."

"Yes, that's what I understood. Were you aware that he has died?"

"Yes, some former colleagues e-mailed me about it shortly after it happened. He was shot, I understand."

"That's correct. Would you be willing to talk with me about what you know about him?"

"Sure."

"Dean Steinman, as our conversation may be long, I'd be willing to drive up to the Twin Cities, where I believe you live, to discuss Dr. White with you, at your convenience of course."

"That would be fine if you think it is the best way to proceed. I will be tied up with family from Thursday on, but would be happy to talk with you in the next couple of days, or after the first."

"I could drive out there tomorrow."

"My schedule is very light this week, so tomorrow afternoon would be fine."

"If you're comfortable seeing me in your office at the University of Saint Paul, I could be there about two p.m. I believe it's about a five hour drive?"

"Two is fine. Yes, it is about five hours. I will be happy to give you directions, with some shortcuts."

"You don't mind seeing me in your office?"

"No, of course not. If you are wearing a uniform and carrying a gun, it may raise some eyebrows."

"Don't worry, I'm plain clothes. I'll just take the interstate to the twin Cities, and shouldn't have any trouble finding the Dean's office. Look for me at two."

"OK. I am in Frederick Hall. See you at two."

The conversation left me a little uneasy. I first had to explain to Sue why the Outagamie County Sheriff's Office wanted to talk with me, and to alert her that I was going to be "interviewed" the next day. (I avoided using the word "questioned.") Jameson had given no suggestion that he thought I was anything more than a former colleague of the dead professor. But he knew where I worked, and he wanted to talk with me in person and at length, and was willing to drive five hours to see me, so he certainly expected or at least hoped to learn something useful from me. On the phone I had found him friendly, well spoken, and rather passive. There was nothing intimidating about him. Nonetheless I spent a good part of the next morning rehearsing mentally questions he might ask and my answers to them. I figured that this was a very good occasion to put into practice what I had learned from Laura Higgins about my poor performance in the deposition for the White lawsuit. I should be very straightforward in my answers, but not answer more than was asked. Jameson would be fishing, and I certainly should not give him information he doesn't ask for. And it would be fine to say "I don't know" or "I don't remember" whenever that is appropriate. Of course the history of my interactions with White was fresh in my mind because of the lawsuit, so I needed to be upfront about that. Jameson would surely know about the lawsuit.

Jameson showed up at two sharp. He was younger than I expected, nicely dressed, could have been a sales rep, or a college professor. We sat down on the two armchairs in front of my desk. I had left the lawsuit documents conspicuously on my desk in the event I needed to consult something to refresh my memory. He began courteously.

"Thank you, Dean Steinman, for taking the time to see me. I won't hide from you the fact that we're baffled by this case. We believe that Peter White was murdered, but have no leads. So any information we can get from you, however unimportant you may think it is, may be helpful. We are looking for someone who had a real motive to kill him."

"I'll be glad to tell you everything I know about Pete White. But, one of my former colleagues told me there was some speculation it might have been an accident, a stray bullet from an early morning hunter."

"We briefly entertained that theory, and did nothing to discourage those who wanted to believe that, but from the very start our ballistic examination suggested otherwise. We have interviewed dozens of hunters who were out in the area in the forty-eight hour period during which he was killed, and we're convinced that none of them could have been that irresponsible and that stupid. No, we are convinced that some person or persons deliberately stationed themselves in the clearing waiting for White to appear in his kitchen, and then shot him intentionally."

"Wow."

"That's how people in the academic world have tended to respond to this information."

"Yeah, that is not how we usually settle our disagreements. It is a lot easier to imagine this as an accident."

"Dean Steinman, I have interviewed dozens of people who knew Peter White, and not one person would say they actually liked him. Did you like him?"

"You know, I did for a while. We got along pretty well in the first couple of years, and then he just became too difficult and too offensive. "

"I have heard that too. What did you like about him at first?"

"Well, I guess I am always prepared to like people until they give me reason not to. I had been told that he was demanding and unreasonable. But in our first encounter he actually responded in a very reasonable manner to the solution I proposed to the issue that had brought us together: a conflict between himself and another faculty member who both wanted to teach the same course."

"And how far did your friendship go"?

"'Friendship' is perhaps overstating it. We could discuss business matters civilly. We had some personal and social interactions. At one point he wanted to organize a public lecture and reception, paying for it himself. And I helped him with that, and it was a nice evening. The most social we ever got was once I invited him to have lunch with me. Purely social. Also, one summer when my son needed to take a college level math course, I recommended he take White's intro to calculus, and that went well."

"What soured the relations?"

"That's easy to pinpoint. We had gotten along well because I tended to give him everything he asked for. But in '94, Tom Summers became Acting Dean of the campus, and he wanted me to be more hard-nosed. I discussed with Summer several travel and schedule requests White had made, and Summers told me to say no. As soon as I started saying no to White, our relations soured."

"Did you hate Pete White?"

"Hate? No. I don't think anyone hated him. People disliked him.

Some may have feared him or at least found him threatening. Almost everyone found him annoying, including me."

"Did you fear him?"

"No. I certainly preferred not to have contact with him. When I had to, I found it distasteful. He was rude and unreasonable, and took up time that I would rather have spent on good, productive issues. Fearing implies that he could do something to hurt me, and he really couldn't. But he could make my life uncomfortable."

"Did you ever wish he was dead?"

"No. I wished he would go away. I know he wanted to move to another campus, and I wanted that to happen. But I didn't wish him harm."

"Are you sorry he is dead?"

"Interesting question. Not particularly. I worry about the harm that might cause his children, but I believe his wife had custody of them anyway."

"How much do you know about his relationship with his wife?"

"Very little. We had heard she was divorcing him, and that he was making it hard. I barely knew her, but had the feeling she was smart and a lot nicer than he was."

"Did you ever discuss his marriage with White?"

"No."

"Can you think of anyone who would have wanted Peter White dead?"

"I know a lot of people who disliked him and feared him, and wished he would go away. But they are all academics, and I guess I like to think that we all have enough altruism and humanity not to wish that someone would die."

"You say you are not particularly sorry he is dead. Do you imagine there are others who feel that way?"

"I do imagine that."

"Who?"

"This may be unfair, but I can't help feeling that all of the administrators of the University of Wisconsin who were inconvenienced by the frivolous lawsuits that he brought against us are not unhappy to see that that problem has been eliminated. I think there are several faculty at the Madison and Lakeside Campuses who felt that he was a real thorn in their sides and are relieved that that thorn has been removed. Does that sound terribly callous?"

"No. It's honest, and it conforms to what most of your former colleagues have told me. I've read the lawsuit depositions and understand fully how you and others felt about White. But is there anyone in particular who would be more relieved and happy to have this thorn removed?"

"Certainly Mary Gregory, and Peter Gordon, my replacement at Lakeside. Mike Fleck. Larry Osborne. Anthony Russo. Any surprises there?"

"Osborne maybe. I need to ask you this, Dean Steinman: can you account for your whereabouts during the time frame when White was murdered?"

"I think so. I was here, I believe. But what is the exact time frame?"

"The coroner says he was probably murdered between six a.m. on the morning of Monday, November 30, and six p.m. on the following day."

"Here, let me look at my calendar... I was in the office all day both those days, with several meetings each day."

"What did you do that Monday night?"

"Hmm. According to my schedule, I had a meeting at four with one of my department chairs. That would have ended at four-thirty or so, after which I probably came by the office to see if there were any messages before going home. Monday night? I think I watched the Monday night football game. It was the period when I was writing promotion recommendations, and I remember now I wrote some recommendations while watching the game. Then went to bed."

"Who was playing?"

"Let me think... the Monday after Thanksgiving... I believe that was the Denver Bronco game when Elway threw four touchdown passes to go ahead of Johnny Unitas, and keep them undefeated. I don't remember who the opponent was."

"Can anyone confirm that you went home?"

"Hmm... I seem to remember I got a Burger King Whopper in Saint Paul. Would they remember me? I don't think I talked with anyone else."

"What about the recommendations you wrote that night? Are they dated?"

"Yes. I probably dated them that day."

"Did you write them on a computer?"

"Yes. My personal laptop."

"Sorry to have to ask those questions. You seem to have found another way to remove the thorn from your side. But one never knows."

"It's all right, I understand. I assume you have asked just about everyone at the campus the same question?"

"Pretty much. I didn't talk much to Osborne. I should probably try him again."

"That seems unlikely to me. I know he didn't like White. And he is a bit of an odd duck. But a gentle soul, I believe."

"I'll leave you my card, Dean Steinman, and I encourage you to call me if you have any further thoughts on the matter."

"Of course. And don't hesitate to call me if you think of any further information I can provide."

"I will. Oh yeah, one other question... This may sound silly, but I have asked it of everyone else I have interviewed: Do you know how to shoot a rifle?"

"Hmm... A little bit. I had a BB gun when I was a kid. My cousin once took me rabbit hunting when I was a teen, and showed me how to shoot a .22. And actually, just a couple of months ago, I had a skeet shooting lesson. I belong to a tennis club, and at a cookout in September, one of our members brought his skeet shooting equipment, and several of us took a turn."

"Were you any good?"

"I actually hit one skeet. But everyone watching said it was luck."

"OK. Well, thank you again for talking with me. See you again."

"And good luck to you. I am curious to see how this turns out."

"Yeah, me too. So long."

After seeing him to the door, and exchanging a few pleasantries with Sue about my ordeal, I sat down behind my desk and ran through the conversation in my head. He obviously had to take me seriously as a possible suspect. But his asking about the football game was a bit aggressive. And then the question about knowing how to shoot a gun was a surprise, but he did say he had asked everyone else the same question. What did he possibly learn from our conversation? He had to conclude that I had no real alibi, that I might very well have driven to Lakeside and back during that night. But he also confirmed that I had no motive – I had found another way to remove the thorn from my side, as he put it. And he also had to conclude that I do not fit the profile of a murderer. I thought I had been pretty open, relaxed, and forthcoming. I even told him more than I had to about my rifle shooting experience. I avoided appearing overly prepared by letting him suggest that the promotion reports would be computer dated, and then pretending not to remember that the Broncos had been playing the Chargers that night. He couldn't rule me out as a suspect. But I certainly had done nothing to encourage his suspicions.

Two

Jameson came back two weeks later, on January 5. He had called the day before, and said he wanted to talk with me again. That of course aroused a lot of curiosity and anxiety. He showed up that Tuesday afternoon, at two p.m.

"Thank you, Dean Steinman, for agreeing to see me again. This shouldn't take too long. Our investigation has evolved somewhat, and it has raised some new questions. I'd like to find out what you know about Peter White's personal life?"

Nothing threatening about this beginning, I thought. I relaxed some, but not entirely. "Actually, very little. I met his wife on a couple of occasions. I think I mentioned the public lecture he gave, and she was there and we chatted a bit. I had seen his two children, a boy and a girl, around campus on a couple of occasions."

"You told me that you had invited him to lunch once, and that on that occasion it was strictly social. What did you talk about?"

"Hmm... Good question. I remember that we went into a restaurant and ran into the man who had preceded me as Associate Dean. I had never met him, so there were introductions, and then when White and I sat down finally, we talked a lot about the campus ten years earlier when White had first arrived. Then, later in the conversation, he wanted to know about my family, I remember. He also wanted to tell me what he thought about all of our colleagues, and specifically warned me not to trust certain individuals and groups."

"That may be useful. Whom did he particularly seem to mistrust?"

"The engineering and science faculty as a whole. There was a lot of tension between him and them. All of the science and engineering students had to go through the calculus sequence and differential equations, and White saw himself as a gatekeeper for those programs."

"Gatekeeper?"

"Yes, as the person who could decide which students were good enough to continue, based on their performance in math."

"Oh, I see. Did you and White ever invite each other to your homes?"

"I think I did invite him to some party at my house once. He said he was honored to be invited but had a conflict. He never invited me to his home."

"Did you know where he lived?"

My internal alarm went off. Had all of this questioning been contrived just to find out if I knew the location of White's apartment? I continued on in the same neutral tone, "No, I didn't. I think I was aware he used to live in a house somewhere in Lakeside, but then I had heard through a secretary's gossip that his wife was filing for divorce and had kicked him out, and he had moved into an apartment somewhere. Through the same gossip I heard that at the school where his kids were enrolled, he was not allowed on the premises."

"You never talked with him about any of this?"

"No, by this time our relations had soured, and we talked only when necessary and only about business, usually he was asking for money for something."

"Did you know about the woman he was seeing in Chicago?"

"Just what I read in the deposition. Is that perhaps a fruitful line of inquiry?"

"We of course followed up with that, looking for a jealous husband or lover. Nothing."

"Inspector Jameson, you began by saying the investigation had evolved. In what direction?"

I had the feeling he looked at me while performing a mental calculation before going on. "We think first of all that we have narrowed the time of death." He paused, I imagined waiting for a reaction from me. Seeing none, he went on:

"I think I told you that the coroner could be no more precise than an estimate that White had died between six a.m. on Monday, November 30, and six p.m. on Tuesday, December 1. As you may remember, he was wearing pajamas and drinking a glass of milk while standing by the refrigerator in the kitchen. We had therefore assumed that he might have been shot while preparing breakfast on either Monday or Tuesday morning. But when we re-interviewed his wife, she said that during their life together, he almost always took a shower and got dressed before eating breakfast, and that he drank coffee at breakfast. She went on to tell us that he had a ritual of going down to the kitchen just before going to bed for a glass of milk. And for that, he was often already in his pajamas. It appears then that he was shot in the midst of his nighttime ritual, and so we place the time of the murder at between ten and twelve p.m. on Monday, November 30."

"Sounds plausible. And how does that effect your investigation?"

Again he paused, and his glance sharpened for a second. "We have reviewed our notes from the interviews with all possible suspects, and there are only two for whom we do not have confirmable affirmations that they were somewhere else with someone else at that time."

I had seen this coming and grinned. "Who is the other?"

"Larry Osborne."

"Well, if I were in your shoes, I guess I would consider me a more likely murderer than Larry. I assume you have talked with him at length?"

"Yes, and your assessment of him as a 'gentle soul' is certainly accurate. But we have been working with profilers, and you both present some interesting personality characteristics."

"Before you go on, inspector. Let me address one of my intellectual characteristics which has occasionally caused some misunderstanding in personal relationships. For some reason, I have often refused to say things which I think are obvious, things like, 'I love you,' or 'I am sorry,' or 'I believe you.' I think you can see how those omissions might cause a misunderstanding. In this case, the obvious thing which I should not omit saying is, 'I did not kill Pete White.'"

Jameson gave me a friendly grin. "So that I won't be guilty of the same characteristic, Dean Steinman, let me add, 'I believe you.' But let me share with you some of the information from our profilers. Yes, Osborne is a gentle soul, and as such is unlikely to commit murder. But our literature teaches us that everyone is capable of committing a murder."

Somewhat reassured by Jameson's professed belief in my innocence, I took interest in his theoretical exposition. "Everyone"?

"Well, almost everyone. It seems to be in our genes, but of course to different degrees. On one end of the spectrum, there are violent, psychotic people who kill easily. On the other end are loving, altruistic, peaceful people we would not ordinarily expect to be capable of murder, but we have documented stories of mothers and fathers under extreme conditions killing to protect their children. And in between, there are pretty ordinary people who, feeling the effect of extreme anger – as in road rage – or under the influence of alcohol or drugs, are capable of violence. And then, there are purely intellectual murderers, analytical, calculating people who can rationalize and justify murder, usually for some personal or societal gain."

"Justify murder for societal gain?"

"Sure, the vigilante mentality. In the old west, they would form a posse to avenge some real or imagined crime. Organized crime often operates that way. Michael Corleone's, 'It's business.' Dean Steinman, I need to take you seriously as a suspect."

"OK. Should I contact a lawyer?"

"We are a long ways from the point where I read you your rights and we question you under oath. I will tell you honestly that we have no evidence which connects you to this crime. You have been forthcoming and straightforward. In my two interviews with you, I have detected none of the reactions which we associate with evasiveness. I might have expected a little more reaction from you just now when I told you I take you seriously as a suspect. But you have already alerted me that you sometimes fail to say obvious things. As an extremely intelligent and perceptive individual, that you're not surprised by our suspicion can be taken as a normal reaction."

"Yes, I suppose I could have been more dramatic in protestations of my innocence. But I have already told you sincerely that I did not kill Pete White, and believed you when you said you believed me. Once you told me that there are only two of us who cannot confirm that we were somewhere else, well, I assumed you had to take me seriously. So, your affirmation of that was not a surprise. Incidentally, how come Osborne has no confirmation of his whereabouts? I know he has a wife and son."

"They were both in bed by ten that night. Osborne says he stayed up reading until midnight, and took their dog for a walk. They live just a mile or so from White's apartment."

"So, what is your next step?"

"I'd like to examine your laptop computer, in your presence. You said that you wrote some promotion recommendations that night, while watching Elway and the Broncos. The football part checks out. You didn't seem to remember that it was the Chargers they beat, but I didn't either, and I watched the game too. If your laptop confirms that you wrote promotion recommendations on it that night, well, it seems unlikely that you would have done that while on the road to kill someone in Lakeside, Wisconsin."

"My laptop is here. You can certainly look at it."

"OK. Are the files you wrote that night still on it?"

"I believe so. I copied them to my office desktop computer, but I am pretty sure I left them on the laptop as a backup. Let's look."

I turned on the laptop. When it was fully loaded, with Jameson watching closely, I opened up Windows Explorer to the "Reappointment, Tenure, and Promotions" file under My Documents, organized them by "Date Modified," and pointed to the six files which had been last modified at regular intervals between seven p.m. and eleven p.m. on the evening of Monday, November 30. Each file had as its title the name of a faculty member; each was between two and three pages, and included descriptions of their teaching, research and service contributions, and a summary paragraph with a recommendation. Jameson seemed impressed.

"And you can demonstrate that those reports were actually submitted?"

"I am pretty sure I printed them all out the following morning, signed them, and brought them down to the Vice President's Office. They probably put a time stamp on them. And those reports are kept on file for years."

"I don't think you need to contact a lawyer, Dean Steinman. At this point, all I have is that you might have been motivated to kill Peter White, and that you maybe had the opportunity, if you could have found a way to write those reports while watching a football game and while driving ten hours between five p.m. on November 30 and eight a.m. on December 1. That is pretty slim, and I don't think any prosecutor would encourage me to bring you in for questioning without the slightest bit of evidence. I don't suppose you own a hunting rifle?"

"No, I don't. My son's BB gun may still be in the house, but you would find no other weapons."

"OK. That's all for now. Call me if you think of anything else that may be useful. But I don't expect to need to talk with you again. Have a good day, Dean Steinman."

We shook hands cordially, and he left. After exchanging the usual pleasantries about the visit with Sue, I sat down a bit shakily at my desk and began to relive the entire conversation. I hadn't been sitting at my desk very long when Jeanne Hanratty appeared in my doorway with a curious smile on her face.

"I understand that the Wisconsin police have been here for the second time? What the hell is that all about?"

"You do remember that I told you the math teacher who had brought that lawsuit against the campus was murdered?"

"Yes, I remember that, but what does it have to do with you?"

"Since I knew the guy pretty well, they have been questioning me as part of their investigation. Come on in and sit down; I will tell you all about it?"

"OK. But do they suspect you?"

"Yes and no."

"Yes and no?"

"Yes, because I am one of only two people who had a grudge against the guy, and who has no verifiable alibi for the time of the murder. No, because. as the detective just told me, I no longer had any motivation to kill him, and there is no evidence linking me to the crime. He also seemed impressed by my straightforward answers to his questions."

"But you were living here when he was killed."

"Right, but they think he was killed between ten p.m. and midnight on the night of Monday, November 30, and while I was home that night watching football and writing reappointment and promotion recommendations, I didn't see or talk to anyone who could confirm that I was here and not driving back and forth to Lakeside, Wisconsin, to shoot Peter White."

"Do they think you possibly hated the guy enough to murder him?"

"I have told them that I disliked him – as did just about everyone else on the campus – and that I was troubled by the ability of one rotten apple to spoil the working environment on the campus. The detective mentioned briefly that their profilers suggest that some people are intellectually capable of murdering someone in order to protect society. I guess they thought that could apply to me."

"Why did he come back a second time?"

"I think that because I was one of two plausible perpetrators, he was trying to either get me to say something incriminating, or to confirm his earlier impression that I am an unlikely suspect."

"Trying to get you to say something incriminating?"

"Well, I was just going through our conversation in my head, and realized that while he was being friendly and supportive, he slipped in a question asking me if I knew where White lived, when there is really no reason I would know where he lived."

"He tried to trip you up?"

"Maybe. Maybe the question was innocent."

"Did he really think you might have driven to Lakeside after work on that day, murdered the guy that night, and then you drove home and went to work the next day?"

"It seemed plausible to him, but I think he is now pretty sure that I was really home watching football and writing reports as I told him."

"How did you convince him of that?"

"Well, I remembered things about the football game I watched, and then I could show him on my laptop computer the reports that had been written that night. He could see the date and time they were written."

"What do you know about the other guy?"

"Other guy?

"The other guy who doesn't have a confirmable alibi."

"His name is Larry Osborne. He is a chemistry professor on the campus. He is a pretty quiet and seemingly kind fellow."

"But he had some motive?"

"Well, I had talked about him some in my first interview with the detective. His and White's offices were very near each other, and I knew that White often used him as a sympathetic listener. During the two years that Osborne was chair of the Faculty Rights and Responsibilities Committee of the Campus, White had used that committee as a forum to air his grievances against the administration. I received a couple of official memos from Osborne in response to those grievances, and was concerned about the obvious manipulation of the committee by White for his own purposes. I actually felt bad for Osborne who was caught in the middle."

"Is Osborne capable of murder?"

"I wouldn't think so, but the detective told me that their profilers are willing to consider that almost anyone is capable of murder. And Osborne is somewhat peculiar?"

"In what ways?"

"His personal life – from the little I know about it – seems to be particularly stressful. He sometimes comes across as nervous and insecure. I think the detective must have picked up on that. But I don't really think that he is capable of planning a murder, and then picking up a hunting rifle to carry it out?"

"And are you?"

"Well, according to the detective, I hypothetically am. By the way, I did assure him that I did not kill Pete White, and when he left here, he assured me that he believes me."

"So, who did?"

"Good question. I obviously have asked myself that question and can't help wondering if it won't eventually come out that White was involved in some affairs that might have brought him into contact with some sordid people."

"Do you have any reason to suspect that?"

"I know his wife left him and then issued some kind of restraining order so that he couldn't get close to their children. So she seems to think him capable of kidnapping. I have heard he has debts, but I don't know much about that, except that creditors sometimes called his office looking for him. And then I learned from reading the depositions that he is involved with a woman who lives in the Chicago area."

"Did you tell the police about all that?"

"I think they already know all that. I know at least that they have followed up on the Chicago woman."

"Do you expect they will be back again to talk with you?"

"Inspector Jameson just told me that he doesn't expect to be questioning me anymore. We'll see..."

PART THREE: Surprises!

One

It was late in the afternoon of Friday, January 8, that I got an e-mail from Steve Weston: Larry Osborne had confessed to the murder of Peter White. I became numb and tingly all over as I read the e-mail. I wanted to call Steve right away, but I was afraid that something in my voice would give away my real thoughts and emotions. I wanted to know more. In vain I searched on-line to see if any news service had picked up the story. The big question for me was "Would the police believe him?"

Was I surprised that Osborne had confessed to a crime he didn't commit? Not completely. I of course hadn't at all foreseen that. But now that it had apparently happened, I thought I understood. I knew Larry was an intelligent but unhappy man. He was a good teacher, but a bit too introverted and unsociable to interact easily with students. He delivered coherent, organized lectures, but had little patience with lazy or inept students. He had modest success as a scholar, writing a paper every other year that usually got published in a scholarly journal. He was unsatisfied with his professional accomplishments and bored and depressed by his daily work routine. I had once suggested to him that he needed counseling. I feared he was vaguely suicidal.

In my conversation with Jameson, I had speculated that Osborne was a possible but unlikely suspect. I knew that Osborne disliked White, and was particularly uncomfortable in the advocacy role he was forced to play as chair of the Rights and Responsibilities Committee with respect to White's complaints. I imagine he at first was delighted to learn of White's death, then felt guilty about his delight. That guilt might have fed on him to the point of spurring him to a public gesture of self-immolation. At the same time, he might have welcomed prison as a way out, a passive suicide. The confession had possibly been part of a negotiation that spared him any consideration of a death penalty, and perhaps also guaranteed him a minimum security prison. He might have envisioned a long prison term as a comfortable retirement and escape from a life he hardly enjoyed.

I also reflected that Osborne was smart enough and meticulous enough (an organic chemist) to convince the police he was the assassin. In the two months since the murder, he had certainly been able to familiarize himself with all of the publicly known evidence, and had also learned as much as he could during his interviews with Jameson, so that he could present himself as the murderer.

So… What was I to do?

Two

I don't remember when the idea that I visit Osborne in prison first occurred to me. It seemed like a reckless reaction, and the more I thought about it, the more reckless it seemed. But I couldn't chase the idea; it obsessed me, and lured me into some reassuring but false suppositions. He was a colleague, and if he had been hospitalized as the result of an illness or an accident, wouldn't I go visit him? If he were grieving the death of a family member, wouldn't I pay a courtesy call? (That was a surprisingly consistent custom of administrators at the campus.) Wouldn't avoiding him at this point appear as cold indifference or the abandonment of a person in trouble? In reality, Osborne and I had never been particularly close. He had been hospitalized once during my tenure as dean, and I had not visited him. Since I no longer worked at the campus, I had no professional responsibility to visit a former colleague in trouble. There was a strong possibility that he would be embarrassed by my visit. How could I explain to him that I wanted to see him now, when I had never demonstrated any particular desire to see him at any other time of our mutual acquaintance?

Over several days I entertained conflicting thoughts, until finally, because I couldn't get Osborne out of my mind, I decided to drive down to Riverdale, on Saturday, January 16, to visit him in the Outagamie County Correctional Facility where he was being held. (The *Riverdale Post Tribune* carried daily updates of the unfolding story, so I knew he had been incarcerated there within hours of his dramatic appearance in the Sheriff's Office on January 8, to confess to the crime.) I had called the prison and learned that there were open visiting hours between one and four p.m. on Saturday afternoons. I had decided not to alert Osborne beforehand of my intent to visit him, mainly because I could always then change my mind if I got cold feet or convinced myself that this visit was indeed foolish or reckless. I left at eight that Saturday morning, had lunch at the Harmony Café in Riverdale, and arrived at the prison just before two p.m. During the drive and at lunch, I rehearsed my questions for him. I really wanted to know why he had confessed to a crime I knew he hadn't committed, but I wasn't going to let slip any hint that I knew he was innocent. So I would question him about his motivation for the crime, and how he claimed to have done it.

After I registered as a visitor, I was ushered through a metal detector and patted down before being shown into the visitors' area. I had visions of what the visitors' room might be like, gleaned from old movies and TV shows; so I imagined we would be separated by a glass barrier and have to communicate through a telephone, with other visitors and inmates crowded around us. It was in fact a much more comfortable arrangement. I was shown into a small cheerfully painted cubicle with three armchairs. It appeared that our conversation would be private, although there were three TV cameras covering every corner of the room. I waited there for about five minutes, until finally the heavily armored door opened noisily, and Osborne, wearing faded denim jeans and a denim shirt, came into the room, and an invisible guard closed the door behind him.

I stood and offered him my hand. He grinned and accepted it tentatively, and I thought I detected something resembling an ironic smirk on his face. "I've been expecting you, Paul."

His demeanor and his words sent something like an electric shock through me. I let nothing of my emotions show, and turned towards him with what I thought would be a blankly inquisitive expression, and offered lamely, "Of course, Larry, I have been worried about you, and wanted to offer my moral support. I can't imagine what you have been going through..." But I didn't get to the end of that sentence before I saw that Larry was laughing, not just laughing because he found something funny, but laughing mockingly and scornfully at me!

"Paul, before you get too far into your phony protestations of compassion and solidarity, let me tell you a little anecdote. You need to know first of all that the police were perfectly willing to believe that I was able to sneak out of the house and murder White at midnight, because I live only a half mile from his apartment complex, and my wife and son are used to hearing me go out between ten-thirty and midnight to walk the dog, which I do almost every night, especially..." and here he paused dramatically, with a sharp glance, upturned eyebrows, and a return of the ironic smirk, "especially on warm summer nights like in late June."

I couldn't believe what I was hearing but still managed to control my facial expression. "Yes, last June 25, my Irish Setter Kelly and I went out for our walk in the woods, about eleven o'clock. As we approached the area behind the Forest Grove apartment, we stopped and watched as a Subaru Legacy pulled into the lot. I immediately recognized it, and curious to see what you were doing there at that time of night, I retreated back into the woods with Kelly. I followed you from a distance to the clearing in front of White's apartment complex, saw you watching his kitchen window until he appeared, and then saw you pretend to shoot him..."

There was obviously no way I could dispute Osborne's account. All I did was raise my eyebrows and wait to see what he would say next.

"Don't worry, Paul. I am not going to tell anyone what I saw that night. Probably no one would believe me anyway. You know, after White was shot, I thought momentarily that it was my duty to go to the police with what I had seen, but there was no reason they would believe me. You could just deny it, and the only result would have been to draw attention to myself, as if I were pointing the finger at you to avoid being suspected. From my conversations with Jameson and the other police inspectors, I know that you left no clues behind that would link you to the crime. I did hear that your account of your activities during the night of the crime cannot be verified, but since you were hundreds of miles away that afternoon and the next morning, well, all I can say is 'Bravo, well done!'"

"Larry, what on earth led you to confess?"

"Good question. Put yourself in my position. I knew you were planning to murder Peter White. And I did nothing to stop you. Even if I lacked the courage to confront you directly, I could have sent you an anonymous letter, describing what I saw the night of June 25. I think that would have stopped you, wouldn't it?"

As I made no response, he went on. "I understand, Paul, that you don't want to say anything incriminating. I am sure that these rooms are not bugged, and I obviously don't have any kind of recording device. I respect your desire to maintain an innocent façade, even with me, who knows that you did it. That's fine. Paul, I knew that my confession would draw you here. You are a good, kind man. You are concerned about me, and I am grateful. You probably thought that the crime would go unsolved, that no one would be arrested, that perhaps the hypothesis of the careless, anonymous hunter would carry the day. But let me get back to your question, why did I confess?"

"The truth is I did feel that I was an accomplice. I knew you were planning to kill Pete White, and I did nothing to stop you, to warn him or to warn the police. So, technically, I do carry some guilt. But, Paul, I am not particularly sensitive to that guilt. I took pleasure in the knowledge that you were planning to kill him. I hated him! Why would I try to stop you? Would you believe that I admired you for the intent, and admired you even more when you carried it out. Now, when Detective Jameson told me that there were only two suspects whose alibis could not be confirmed, I worried about you. I knew you had left no clues, and knew too that in his interrogation of you, you would give nothing away. But I did see the possibility of a chink in your armor: me! I was potentially your Achilles heel. If they began to suspect me, you might feel honor bound to protect me by confessing. Jameson knew that; he really did suspect you, and he had assessed your character and knew that you would potentially step forward to protect me. So, I intervened proactively."

Osborne paused at this point to let the weight of his words sink in. I was moved, and let it show. "Larry, what about you? What about your wife? What about your son?"

"We are all taken care of, Paul. Our house is paid for, and my TIAA-CREF pension fund has surged in the last five years, so there will be enough income for Shelly and James to live comfortably. Besides, I don't expect to be in here very long. They have already sent around a team of psychologists to evaluate me, and my lawyer is probably going to enter an insanity plea. I have to admit that Pete White really did drive me nuts. I lacked the courage to stand up to his bullying harassment. I lost sleep over his manipulation of me as chair of the R&R Committee. I hated the memos he forced me to write. I sometimes locked myself in my office and cried. Pretty nutty, isn't it?"

"I certainly understand that. He had a very strong impact on all of us. We can all be grateful that he is gone."

"Thanks to you!"

"This is very awkward for me, Larry. Don't you worry about going through the rest of your life branded as a murderer?"

"You mean 'applauded as a murderer.' You might be aware by now that there is an internet Larry Osborne fan club. I get daily e-mails and letters congratulating me for standing up to a bully. In the prison here, I have hero status. My wife tells me she is treated with respect almost everywhere she goes. This is the ultimate 'win-win' situation for the two of us, Paul."

"I really don't know what to say, Larry, and I am not sure what I should be doing to help you. Believe me when I say that I want to help you. I am surprised to find you serenely accepting of everything engulfing you, Larry. And that makes it hard for me to imagine what I can do... So, I guess there is nothing left for me to do but to thank you. Would you like me to visit you again? Or maybe Shelly and James?"

"Probably not a good idea, Paul. Maybe after I'm out. I am very glad we had this talk. I assume you will be following closely how things go. I sincerely hope there will be no more surprises for you."

"Me too, Larry. Thanks, and good luck!"

"See you around, Paul."

Three

I left the prison, my head awhirl with conflicting emotions. I looked at my watch, just two-thirty. I had plenty of time to drive into Lakeside where I was supposed to meet Steve Weston for coffee at three-thirty, so I sat in my car in the prison parking area for nearly thirty minutes, reviewing my conversation with Osborne, obsessed with the question of what would happen if they figured out that his confession was bogus. Under pressure, would he crack and implicate me?

Steve Weston was my closest friend among the campus faculty. He had chaired the search committee that had hired me, and since he was a professor of English, and had an interest in theatre, we had strong intellectual ties, and had worked together on some curricular projects. It was Steve who had first "informed me" of White's death, and had since that time kept me informed of the progress of the investigation. I had e-mailed him that I was going to pay a courtesy call on Osborne, and he had invited me to join him for a cup of coffee.

I arrived at the Dunkin' Donuts at three-twenty, and Steve was already there waiting for me. After exchanging a few pleasantries about our families, Steve plunged right in: "So what do you think, now that you have talked with Larry?"

"What do you mean?"

"Paul, no one on campus believes he did it."

Alarms went off in my brain, and my vision swam for an instant. This was one more unpleasant surprise, and I had to fight once again to keep my face emotionless.

"Really?"

"We have known the guy for twenty years. No way..."

"Well, he seems to have convinced the police."

"For now. No one really knows how he was able to lead the police right to the spot from which the bullets were fired. That gave his story tremendous credibility. They had to lock him up after that. But the story of how he got rid of the rifle is about to start leaking."

"I don't know anything about that."

"No, it wasn't in the paper. He claims he borrowed some sulfuric acid from the chem lab and dissolved it over two days. But Shaefer has been telling people on campus that they never stocked enough acid to come close to dissolving a rifle, and that as far as he can tell, none is missing. And remember, it is Shaefer who has been doing all the ordering of chemicals for the past ten years."

"Wow! This is all news to me. I have to admit that I was stunned when you wrote me that Larry had confessed to the murder. But the more I thought about it, the more I succumbed to the idea that he might just have been crazy enough to do it. I have to say that just now while visiting him, I got the distinct impression that he was enjoying the notoriety of his new status, and not at all dreading the consequences to himself or to his family."

"Yeah, we have all been talking about that."

"So, what do you think is going to happen?"

"Just this week, Shaefer told the police about the sulfuric acid. They didn't react much, but we have been hearing through Gary Baker, who has friends on the force, that the case seems to be unraveling. The only things that point to Larry are his confession, and that he pinpointed the exact spot from which the police ballistic analysis showed the bullets had been fired. And as for his motive, well, lots of us hated White just as much or even more than he did... I understand, Paul, that you have been questioned."

"Yeah, twice. It turns out that Larry and I were the only suspects who didn't have verifiable accounts of where we were at the time of the shooting."

"But weren't you in the Twin Cities?"

"Yes, but that day, I didn't really have any recorded contact with anyone from the time I left the office at five, until the next morning."

"So, you might have driven down here after work, shot White, and then driven back home in time to get to work the next morning?"

"That apparently was a hypothesis."

"Which doesn't really make sense, since you don't work here anymore, and have no reason to care whether White lives or dies."

"Except for my enduring affection for you guys. So, if the case against Osborne crumbles, what will the police do?"

"Are they still interested in you?"

"I don't think so. After my second round with Detective Jameson, he seemed pretty convinced that I had been home that night watching football and writing reappointment recommendations. They are still on my laptop, dated at the time of the shooting."

"Except those can be manipulated."

"What do you mean?"

"Don't you remember, we had that plagiarism case in one of my Shakespeare classes? Two roommates each claiming that the other had copied her paper. We looked at their computers to try to determine when each had written her paper. But then Patricia pointed out to us that by resetting the date on your computer, you can manipulate the date and time it stamps on a document."

"Yes, I guess you had pointed that out to me at the time. How did we resolve that case?"

"We never really did. We just gave each of the students a stern warning. Anyway, I am sure the police have lots of reasons to believe you didn't do it."

"I think so. But where are they likely to turn next?"

"They were grateful for Larry's confession, and quite willing to believe him because they really are stumped. Lots of people with motives, but zero clues. They may be willing to go back to the hunting accident theory."

"Which I had the feeling no one really believed to begin with."

"Right."

The conversation gradually moved away from the sensational crime story which had brought us together that Saturday to more general topics such as other professional news, vacations, travel plans, and family. We concluded by agreeing that we needed to get together sometime in the next months, and parted amiably, about four-thirty.

As I began the four hour ride back to the house in Saint Paul, I revisited both conversations, and found myself increasingly alarmed by the new information I had. First of all, Larry Osborne knew I had killed Pete White! I had somewhat recovered from the initial shock of that revelation with Larry's reassurance that he would never tell anyone, and the likelihood that no one would believe him if he did. But now, knowing that the police did not believe that Larry was the murderer, and were about to release him, I had to worry that they would press him with questions about how he had been able to identify the precise spot from which the bullets had been fired. That had to intrigue them.

And then there was Steve's innocent reminder that he knew and had once pointed out to me that the time and date stamp on a Word document could be manipulated. If he knew that, then Police Inspector Jameson also possibly knew it. He hadn't said anything about that to me, which, upon reflection, was more worrisome than if he had. He was maybe saving that for a later surprise. I wondered if the changes I had made to adjust the date/time stamp left any record. How could I find that out without arousing suspicion? Maybe I needed to get rid of the computer? How could I do that?

Ultimately, I could console myself with the knowledge that I had left no clues and had aroused no suspicion. Even if Larry were to admit that he had seen my rehearsal of the crime, there was a strong likelihood that no one would believe him, and it would be impossible for anyone to prove that he had really seen my on that June night. I could deny it, and suggest that Larry's overactive imagination had conjured that up, as he knew I was the only remaining suspect. I could even imply subtly that Larry knew the spot because he was in some way an accomplice and was trying to protect someone else.

I thought about the rifle, now still buried in Brown Creek State Park. I suddenly felt a strong temptation to drive by the spot since it was not far out of my way home, just to make sure it was as I had left it. Why not, I thought? It was five o'clock and dark when I exited onto Route 54, then took Brown Creek Road to the park entrance. Seeing no other cars in either direction, I pulled into the park entrance road, then stopped and gasped. Construction vehicles lined the roadway; there were stacks of storm sewage pipes on the left edge of the pavement where a wide ditch had been opened. A few construction workers still lingered, as they had apparently just stopped work for the day. I did a quick U-turn and headed back to the highway before anyone could notice me. "That's all I need," I thought to myself, and continued on home without any further stops.

Four

Three days passed. I had seen in the on-line editions of the *Post Tribune* that Osborne was indeed released, and heard from Weston that he was seeing a therapist and had been placed on indefinite leave from his teaching post at the campus. I was tempted to call him, but thought that would be dangerous. He was certainly being watched; would they also tap his phone? I couldn't risk that.

I tried to get the whole business out of my head, but the loose ends kept haunting me: There was a man who knew that I had killed Pete White, Inspector Fred Jameson possibly knew that I could have manipulated the time/date stamp in my laptop, and perhaps the rifle had been uncovered. There was no way to have any certainty on that latter point. There was no reason such a discovery would be announced. If the construction workers had uncovered it, would they report it to the police? Would the police in Waupaca associate the uncovered rifle with a murder in Lakeside?.

I kept waiting for a proverbial "other shoe" to fall, and finally it did, on Wednesday, January 20. Mid-morning, my secretary called out to me that Fred Jameson was on the line. I picked up the phone anxiously.

"Good morning, Inspector Jameson. How are you this morning?"

"Fine, thanks, I hope I am not catching you at a bad time?"

"No, this is fine, what can I do for you?"

"Well, I have some business that'll take me up to your part of the world tomorrow, and I was wondering if we could have another chat."

"Sure. Have there been some new developments in the White case?"

"Oh, nothing particularly dramatic. I imagine you know about the false confession from Larry Osborne, his arrest and subsequent release. That was on one hand a distraction, but on the other, it has given us some new information to follow up. It raised some interesting new questions."

"Well, I will be glad to talk with you tomorrow. What time, do you think?"

"Let's make it three o'clock. Do you want to meet again in your office?"

"That's fine."

"OK, I will see you at three o'clock, tomorrow, Dean Steinman."

"Good, see you then."

Well, if Fred Jameson was purposefully trying to arouse my anxiety, he probably couldn't have been any more effective. What business could he possibly have in "my part of the world?" Was he coming up to Menomonie to question the gun dealer who had sold me the M-1? Why hadn't I thought to buy the gun at some gun show far away from here? The geographic proximity was enough to point a finger at me. And then there was the vague assertion that Osborne's confession had revealed some new information. It could easily be conjecture about how Larry had been able to lead them to the exact spot from which the bullets were fired.

I had done nothing about the laptop. I had looked on-line for any websites that might discuss the time/date stamp on a PC, and found nothing dealing specifically with the question whether my manipulation of it had left a trace. Getting rid of the laptop would be suspicious, as would removing those files. But, mightn't it be better to do something that might appear suspicious rather than leaving some very damning evidence? I thought it through, and decided that the most prudent course of action was to do nothing. In the event that the manipulation was noticeable, I had a cover story ready. I would remember that back in early November, I had bought a new battery for the laptop, and that I had sometime later reset the date and time. I would even make sure that the laptop was with me in my office, in case he wanted to look at it again.

In anticipation of his visit, I read carefully the on-line *Post Tribune*, looking for any reference to the murder. Other than the release of Osborne from prison, there had been no newsworthy events or announcements. I sent Weston a friendly e-mail, asking about Osborne, and wondering if there was anything new in the investigation. He told me Osborne probably wouldn't be returning to work until the fall, mainly, as he explained, to give the notoriety he had achieved time to die down. There were no new leads he was aware of, and people were gradually moving on to other subjects of faculty lounge gossip.

In order to appear to be calm and relaxed when Jameson appeared, at about five minutes to three, I invited my secretary Sue Renquist into my office to tell her the story of my phone conversation earlier that afternoon with History Department Chair Bill Campbell. Bill began the conversation by announcing, "Paul, I did it again." Then he went on to confess sheepishly that once again he had made a totally inappropriate comment to a troublesome student, and was sure that we would be hearing from the student's parents. She and I were laughing gaily about it when Jameson appeared promptly at three. He greeted us warmly, and after a bit of polite conversation, she excused herself, and Jameson and I sat, as we had on his previous visits, on the two armchairs in front of my desk. I waited for him to begin.

"Well, since my last visit, the major event in my investigation was of course the confession by Larry Osborne, and then our subsequent determination that he wasn't the perpetrator after all."

I said I was aware of his confession, and then added, since I was sure he already knew this, that I had visited Larry in jail.

"Yes, I was aware of that. I wanted to discuss with you the conversation you had with Osborne, because, in all candor, Dean Steinman, while we're quite convinced that Osborne did not commit the murder, we think he may know who did it."

"Might he have been part of a conspiracy?"

"Maybe. Or he might have learned something accidentally. At any rate, he seems to know more than he's willing to tell. By the way, he still claims he did it! So, did he say anything to you that might indicate he knows who did kill Peter White?"

"No, he claimed he did it, and we talked more about why, and what was going to happen to him and his family. By the way, that's the reason I went to see him. While we weren't particularly close when we were colleagues, it is a small campus, and there is a strong feeling of solidarity among faculty and staff. I had met his wife and son, and they seemed to be very close. I really worried about the impact his imprisonment would have on his family. I offered to help." I immediately wished I hadn't volunteered all that. I certainly had no obligation to offer excuses and explanations. But Jameson just nodded and went on.

"You may be aware that the reason we first believed his confession is that he was able to pinpoint the exact location from which the shots had been fired. We are very curious to know how he knew that."

"Obviously, he would know that if he were the murderer. Why are you so sure he isn't?"

"We had our doubts from the beginning because his versions of the events of that night were inconsistent. But the real sticking point was the rifle. He at first told us it was a hunting rifle he had gotten years before from his father, but that didn't pan out ballistically.

And then his story of how he disposed of the rifle didn't convince us either."

"Right, I heard from a friend at the campus that he claimed to have dissolved it in acid."

"Which was feasible, but he couldn't have gotten the necessary quantity from the campus's chemistry lab, as he claimed."

"What did he say when you confronted him with that information?"

"He just sticks to his story. Says he had been storing the acid for months. Getting back to my earlier question, which is the main reason I wanted to talk with you again, did Osborne say anything to you during your twenty minutes of intense conversation with him, which would, now in retrospect, suggest that he did not commit the crime but knows who did."

The phrase "twenty minutes of intense conversation" set off an alarm bell. Certainly, the prison logged visitors, so he could easily have determined from that how long I had been there. But was there something in his tone to suggest that our conversation had been observed? I had assumed that they could not legally listen in on conversations between prisoners and their visitors, but there were video monitors in the room, and I had to wonder if Jameson had been able to study video tapes of our conversation, and if our respective attitudes might have given some hint of what we had said to each other. I furrowed my brow while absorbing the emotion his question provoked, even rubbed my temple as if trying to recall what we had talked about. Finally, I said, "No, I can't think of anything. It seems to me that during our entire conversation there was no question of whether or not he had shot Pete White."

"OK. Do continue to think about your conversation with him. Maybe something will occur to you later."

"Sure."

"Well, I won't keep you any longer. But, I remembered that before the first time we met, you offered to give me directions from Lakeside here. I assume that having made the trip often, you know some shortcuts, instead of taking the Interstate and then Route 10 all the way."

More alarm bells went off, but I remained calm. "Sure, I have a map here, and can show you." I pulled a Wisconsin state highway map out of a desk drawer and opened it over the laptop which I had left conspicuously on my desk. I traced the route for him with a pencil: "To get back to Lakeside more quickly, you should take the Interstate to Eau Claire, then Route 29 to I-39 at Wausau, which you take south past Stevens Point to Plover and then Route 54 to Waupaca. It avoids a lot of traffic."

"OK, and I can certainly find my way home from Waupaca. So, the tricky part appears to be Route 54... Let's see, that goes by Brown Creek State Park. Seems to me though that I heard there is some road construction going on through there now."

My heart sank. He was toying with me. But I remained smilingly calm. "Hmm, I went by there the other day when I visited Larry, and didn't notice any problem."

"OK. Mind if I take the map?"

"No, go right ahead."

He looked at me fixedly for a bit longer than was normal, then smiled, "OK, try to remember anything from that conversation with Osborne that might help us. You know how to reach me."

"I will. Have a good trip back."

After he left, I sat at my desk for a long time. There could be no doubt that he believed I was the murderer, and that he was toying with me. They had undoubtedly found the rifle in the park, and traced it to the seller in Menomonie. I imagined, however, that he had not been either willing or able to provide much information about the buyer, beyond the phony name and address I had given him. It is in the best interest of gun sellers not to notice or remember too much about their buyers. But the fact that the gun had been traced to a seller not far from the Twin Cities area must obviously have piqued Jameson's interest. His reference to construction around Brown Creek State Park was both a tease and a trap. A traveler going straight along Highway 54 would not have seen the drainage work which was after the turnoff into the park. Any confirmation that I was aware of it could have been incriminating.

So what did Jameson know? I tried to imagine in the bleakest possible terms what he might know or suspect. He knew the gun was bought in Menomonie and disposed of in Brown Creek State Park, which is just off my route from Lakeside to the Twin Cities. He knew I had no confirmable alibi, and that the time/date stamp on the reports I supposedly wrote that night could have been manipulated. He had probably seen the video tape of my conversation with Osborne, but had certainly not heard the conversation. He might have guessed that Osborne knew I did it, either because we had planned it together, or because Osborne had accidentally witnessed the shooting (in either case, Osborne would have known the location from which the bullets were fired).

And then there was the map that he asked to borrow! How could a cop not have a state highway map? He wanted a fingerprint sample! I had, I thought, wiped the gun clean, and then I wore gloves the night of the shooting. But might I have somehow left a print on it? Or on something else left at the scene? I was sure I hadn't. Was this maybe just another ploy to increase my anxiety?

So, where did I stand? There was no legal case against me. I had done or said nothing that incriminated me. Visiting Osborne was perhaps imprudent, but it was a calculated risk from which I had picked up useful information, without dangerously incriminating myself. While Jameson probably thought I was guilty, he knew he had no case, and all he could do was to continue to try to trap me into some act that would give me away to the extent he could formally detain me. I was very happy I had not tried to get rid of the laptop; that would have clearly been a suspicious act. I had not flinched when Jameson tried to provoke me with his references to my conversation with Osborne and the construction in the park, or when he asked to keep the map. He probably left here somewhat less certain of my guilt than when he arrived.

So, what would he do next? He would probably try to continue working on Osborne. I really felt I had nothing to fear from that. I didn't think that Osborne would tell what he had seen. And even if he did, his credibility was very suspect, and he could not prove that he had seen me that night. Jameson might ask to examine my laptop. I had my battery change story ready if my manipulation was detectable. He might question some of my colleagues at the University of Saint Paul. Nothing to fear from that either. But I really felt that if I did nothing to arouse any further suspicion, he would have no pretext to question me again or anyone else about me. There were no other clues out there. All I had to do was sit tight.

At that point in my reflection, Sue yelled to me from the outer office that there was a call for me. A woman with an accent, she couldn't understand her name. I picked up the phone.

"Hello, this is Paul Steinman."

"Dean Steinman, this is Veronika Vlesniuk, you don't know me, but I was the fiancée of Peter White."

I was aware that after his separation, Peter had started seeing a woman in Chicago, a mathematician at Northwestern University.

I assumed this must be the woman, and was more intrigued than alarmed that she was calling.

"Yes, Ms. Vlesniuk, I was vaguely aware that Peter was engaged. I am very sorry about your loss. Please let me know if I can do anything to help you."

"Oh, Dean Steinman, I sense that Peter was right about you. He often spoke about you as the one Wisconsin administrator who had both integrity and a good heart."

"I have to say that I am a little surprised to learn that he told you that. Peter and I were often at odds."

"Oh, Peter was at odds with everyone. He was a very difficult man, I know. Dean Steinman, would you be willing to talk with me? That would be very helpful."

"Of course. What do you propose?"

"I would be willing to travel to the Twin Cities to meet with you. I have relatives there I can stay with. I could come this weekend."

"That would be fine. I have no plans for this weekend. I would be pleased to take you out to dinner, perhaps Saturday night?"

"That would be wonderful. I know you must be very curious why I want to talk with you, but it is complicated, and I would rather not talk about it on the phone."

"Of course. My home phone number is (651) 880-7954. Why don't you call me Saturday morning, and we'll arrange where to meet that evening.

"Thank you so much! I am very eager to meet you and talk with you."

I hung up with a strong mixture of emotions. But I sensed that I faced no danger from Veronika Vlesniuk, and that I might learn something useful.

Five

I decided that I wanted to take Veronika to my favorite Saint Paul restaurant, Meritage. I had been there only a couple of times before, and was excited to have a good excuse to return, and of course intrigued to meet and talk with Veronika Vlesniuk.

It is hard for me to understand why I was so eager to meet and talk with her. I had all kinds of good feelings about this, a presentiment that something good would come of our conversation. The favorable opinion she had of me contributed to that feeling, but that was not sufficient to explain the intuitive certainty I had that she would somehow help me through the minefield I was anxiously navigating. Why would I expect this of the woman whose fiancée I had murdered? I really can't explain that.

We talked that Saturday morning, and agreed to meet at the restaurant at eight p.m. The cousins with whom she was staying would drive her there, and I offered to drive her home to them after dinner.

When I entered the Meritage's elegant bar at seven fifty-five, I saw a very fashionably dressed, slim, attractive woman at the bar, sipping a glass of Stoli. She returned my tentative smile and "good evening," and I immediately recognized the charming Eastern European accent of the woman I had spoken to on the phone. She rose, and we introduced ourselves. The Maître D greeted me by name and led us to a table overlooking the restaurant's garden patio, now closed for the season. Soon after we sat down, our waiter brought my single malt on the rocks, and we began the process of getting acquainted. Veronika informed me that, as I had guessed from her name and accent, she was from the Ukraine. She had completed her doctoral studies in mathematics at the National University of the Ukraine, and finding no suitable professional openings in her own country, she had applied to several American universities. As her English was excellent, her studies brilliant, and her area of research – neural networks – much in demand, she had had several offers from US universities, and had ultimately accepted an offer from Northwestern. She had guessed correctly that that University's location in a major US city would lead her to interesting and lucrative consulting opportunities.

Now, I had known that Peter White's specialty was also neural networks, but in our seven years of working together, I had never felt comfortable asking him just was that was all about. I felt immediately at ease with Veronika, however, and emboldened to ask.

"Veronika, I know that research in neural networks is central to the evolution of computer architecture, and software programming. But just how does theoretical research involving mathematical models lead computer engineers and software developers from biological neurons to practical applications."

"Good fundamental question, Paul. And you may be amused to know that it is basically a slow, mundane process of development by trial and error. The question is still being debated just how sophisticated our models need to be in order to mimic animal intelligence. Diagrams of the human brain's neural structure show that it is much too complex to be imitated by computers we have today. But does the human brain really need all that complexity? We have discovered that the answer is 'probably not.' Mathematical neural networks are relatively simplified data-modeling and decision-making tools that can do much of the analyses and calculations of the brain. An artificial neural network made up of simple processing elements can exhibit complex global behavior. We have been continually refining and adding complexity to the first models developed in the 1940s, and the development has led us further and further from the original biological models. Through the process of trial and error we have established practically functioning artificial analytical networks capable of sophisticated classifications, pattern recognitions, data flow control, and behavior projections. The work goes on all over the world now, and the progress is quite stunning."

"I can see how the ability to classify data and to control its flow, and the ability to predict future behavior have the potential to excite government contractors."

"Absolutely! Our work is constantly in demand. I earn far more from my consulting work with government and private contractors than from my university teaching. The field of robotic research has evolved in partnership with the development of neural network research. You are certainly aware of the cliché that armies of the future will be robots equipped with artificial intelligences, and that future air wars will be fought with pilotless airplanes guided from far away by computer operators with joysticks. This is all imminent, and the product of neural network research. And this is a good point, Paul, from which to approach the subject which has brought us together. I am referring of course to the death of my former friend, Peter White."

"In our phone conversation, you referred to him as your fiancée."

"Yes, we often used that expression, but we really had no intention of getting married. Peter and I were professionally and personally associated, and did engage in intimate relations following his legal separation. But that component of our relationship had cooled long before his death."

"I see. Veronika, I have to say that I am a bit at a loss to understand why you want to talk to me about Peter's death. You certainly must know that I have been named in the two legal complaints he filed against the University of Wisconsin, and our relationship was often testy and confrontational."

"Oh, that is the way Peter was. But he really liked and respected you. He respected your intelligence, your honesty, your culture, and your sensitivity."

"While telling the University Human Resources Officer that I was holding him hostage in a burning building?"

"Oh, he really was certifiably insane at that time. I know his illness appeared to many as contrived or at least exaggerated, but he really was quite delusional for a period of several months, largely as the result of fatigue and drugs he was taking. He did have lots of issues with the University, some real, most the result of his delusions. The diagnosis of narcissistic personality disorder and passive/aggressive personality disorder is right on target. And I am afraid too that I must tell you that Peter was a liar, a plagiarist, and an adventurer."

"Not at all what I expected to learn from his 'fiancée.' But what specifically did you want to talk with me about?"

"Paul, the local police investigating Peter's death are way off track. They imprisoned that poor chemistry teacher, and I have heard they may even suspect you! Anyone who has worked in academia knows we don't kill our enemies. We sometimes deny them tenure, or lodge plagiarism and sexual harassment charges against them. We give them crummy office space, deny them travel funds, give them inconvenient teaching schedules – by the way, I am in no way implying that Peter's accusations against you and your colleagues are justified – but, we do not shoot them through the window of their kitchen. That is the work of a wholly different breed."

"What breed would that be, Veronika?"

"In this case, Paul, international arms dealers."

"International arms dealers!? And just what was their interest in Peter White's death?"

"OK, Paul. This is going to sound crazy and romantic, and you may not believe me, but Peter was involved with some dangerous work, and working with some dangerous people. And he ripped them off."

"I guess it doesn't surprise me that he ripped them off. But how did he get involved with these people?"

"Through me, I am sad to say. The Russian Empire is of course dead, and the Russians and Ukrainians are no longer part of a world power whose army threatens the world. So their interest in buying and selling scientific and military secrets is not what it used to be during the cold war. Now, it is even more dangerous. The motivation is not paranoia or patriotism ('same thing' many will say) but greed. Former Soviet scientists and military strategists are willing to sell their knowledge, and international arms dealers have become world-wide brokers of stolen military and scientific knowledge, as well as weapons. You can find their clients in any third world country where oppressed minorities have begun to arm themselves, or in countries where Islamic fundamentalists have organized militarily."

"So Peter's research had military weapons potential?"

"In theory yes, but Peter was a very mediocre scholar. On the other hand, he was a bold bluffer. Those of you at Wisconsin who questioned some of his research accomplishments were right on target. A mediocre researcher, but a skillful plagiarist. You might remember that in the early 90s, he talked your campus into hiring a Chinese mathematician named Siquan Chen?"

"Yes, I remember the guy. White ended up hating him."

"Right. And the reason was quite simple. White had spotted him at an international neural networks conference as an up and coming scholar, whose work was in the same general area as Peter's, but much more sophisticated, with potential application to robotic weaponry. White told people he brought him to your campus as a possible collaborator because Chen lacked adequate support for his research in his home country. In reality, he wanted to steal his research. And he did. He published an article under his own name which was 100% stolen from draft papers that Chen had naively let him read. Chen tried to blow the whistle, but the University botched the investigation and Peter got away with it."

"I remember hearing about that when I arrived at the campus."

"After that, Peter could no longer publish any of Chen's stuff. The word was out among journals in the field to stay away from Peter White. So, he decided to try to sell it. And that is where I became useful to him. We met at an international neural networks conference in Scotland. I gave a paper, and he came up to me afterwards to discuss my work. I found him handsome and charming, we went out for a drink together, and ended up in his hotel room. Incidentally, the University treated him to some very luxurious accommodations. Our relationship developed over time, and he visited me often in Chicago. He was very interested in my consulting business, and asked me to help him establish contacts. I offered to mention him to some of my employers, and half-jokingly mentioned that I had an old friend from Odessa, who was pretty shady, and represented international clients looking to develop software applicable to robotic weaponry. That got him really excited, so I gave him the number of Mikael Vichansky. Mikael at first thanked me for putting Peter in touch with him, but subsequently complained bitterly to me that Peter was an unprincipled liar and cheat, and that he had grossly overstated the importance of the research he was doing, and had tried to sell his clients research results that had been plagiarized from other mathematicians."

"Wow! It is one thing to rip off a poor Chinese mathematician by stealing his research. It is a completely different thing to try to sell that stolen research to international arms dealers. So, you think these guys might have killed him?"

"Of course. I don't know details, but it seems obvious to me. From what I have read and heard from people aware of the investigation, the police are baffled, there are no clues. Sounds like a professional killing to me. And I understand that the police in Lakeside recovered bullets from a Russian Dragunov sniper rifle."

My quickly dropping jaw, and the look of amazement on my face drew a derisive laugh from Veronika. "Yes, I know, we see these things in movies and on TV, but never imagine it can happen in a backwoods place like Lakeside, Wisconsin. Well, Paul, welcome to the global world of international weapons trade."

I struggled to get my voice back, so as to be able to articulate an intelligible question. I sipped from the glass of water before me, with a shaky hand that attracted Veronika's attention.

"Are you all right?"

"I have to admit that I am shocked and incredulous. Have you talked with the police about this?"

"They questioned me right after the killing, as they knew I had been seeing Peter, and they thought that someone connected with me, a jealous ex-husband or ex-lover, might have killed him. At that point, I had suspicions that it was related to Peter's dealing with Mikael and his associates, but didn't say anything. I don't want those guys harboring any resentment of me! Since then, I have become increasingly sure, but still reluctant to go to the police with my suspicions."

"Why are you telling me all this? Do you want me to go to the police with this information?"

"Well, I have heard that you have been questioned by the lead investigator in the case, and I thought you could steer him in that direction, either directly or indirectly. I don't really have a strong interest in the real culprits being brought to justice. I don't think they will be anyway. They are probably out of the country by now. But I do wish they would leave the poor chemistry professor in peace. So, my goal here is to plant a seed with you. It has made me feel better to tell someone like you what I think is going on here. What you do with it is your business."

We spent the rest of the evening talking at first about Peter White, but then moved on to more general issues such as Veronika's earlier life in the Ukraine, and the academic ambience at Northwestern. At eleven p.m., we finished dessert and coffee, and I drove Veronika back to her cousins' home in Minneapolis, and then went straight home, still in a state of shock that there were possibly bullets from a Russian rifle at the murder scene. Just what was going on?

The next day, Sunday, while reading the New York Times in the morning, and then going on a long walk in the afternoon, I kept running through in my head the conversation with Veronika, and then tried to recreate in my mind the scene in the woods in Lakeside the night of November 30. Was it possible that I was not alone? Or was Veronika's hypothesis the product of an over-stimulated imagination? If there really had been bullets from another rifle, then I had to believe that I was not alone. I had to know, and the best way to find out was to ask Inspector Fred Jameson. And my approach to him had been made easier by Veronika's hypothesis.

So, the next afternoon, I called him from work. To my surprise, he picked up the phone immediately on the second ring.

"Jameson here."

"Inspector Jameson, this is Paul Steinman."

"Yes, how are you?"

"I am fine, thanks. Say, you encouraged me to call you if I had any further thoughts on the Peter White murder. And well, I do. Can we talk?"

"Sure, go ahead."

"Over the weekend, I met Veronika Vlesniuk."

"White's girlfriend."

"Right."

"What does she have to say?"

"Well, she has this rather outrageous theory that White was involved, because of his research, with international arms dealers... She says he ripped them off, and that they might have retaliated. As I said, it sounds pretty unlikely to me, but I thought I should pass that along."

"Why did she go to you with that information? "

"This part of it surprised me too. She claims that White had told her favorable things about me, and that I could be trusted. She didn't want to go directly to the police, because she knows some of these people, and doesn't want to be identified as the source of information. Do you take this seriously?"

"Maybe. I will say that there is some evidence that possibly points in that direction. But it may also be a red herring."

"Evidence? "

"Can't say any more about that. Does Dr. Vlesniuk name any names?

"Yes, she spoke of an old friend of hers, a Ukrainian named Mikael Vichansky, who is now involved in shady operations."

"Any other particulars you can share?"

"Apparently White was trying to sell them research done by a Chinese scholar named Siquan Chen."

"All right, well, thanks for bringing that information to me. Have a good day, Dean Steinman."

He hung up, and I held the phone in my hand for several seconds more, absorbing the disappointment of that conversation. I not only didn't get any information, but I got the distinct impression that he didn't want to talk with me, almost as if he were annoyed that I had troubled him with that. I decided that it would make me feel better to discuss this with Veronika, so I called her. She had left me her card on Saturday, so I called her office number, and she picked up almost immediately.

"Hello, this is Dr. Veronika Vlesniuk."

"Hello, Veronika, it's Paul Steinman..."

"Yes, Paul, how are you?"

"I'm OK, but I just called the inspector who is investigating the Peter White murder to tell him about your theory, and, well, he seemed very uninterested."

"I guess I am not surprised, Paul. If they want to steer the investigation in that direction, they will have to deal with a lot of federal agencies, and local police really don't want to do that."

"Federal agencies... like the FBI?"

"Oh, the FBI, the Treasury Department's Alcohol, Tobacco and Fire Arms Division, and possibly even the National Security Agency, because these international weapons dealers are a threat to national security. There is apparently no coordination among them, and they get in each other's way, and in the way of local police. It all works to the benefit of the dealers. I bet your local inspector would rather arrest the wrong guy or drop the investigation completely than get involved with the feds."

"So, he will just ignore the possible link?"

"I am afraid so. But thank you for trying. It doesn't really matter unless they go back after the chemistry professor... or you."

"Say, Veronika. You said there was a rumor that the police had found bullets from a Russian weapon. Just whom did you hear that from?"

"I said more than I should have. But I can trust you. Actually it was Mikael who told me that the murderer was a trained assassin, and that the weapon was a Dragunov sniper rifle. He bragged that the murder was 'signed.' These people are not afraid of the police."

"Veronika, could I talk with Mikael?"

"Not a good idea, Paul. He would know that I have been blabbing about him. And you don't want to get involved with them."

"You are probably right about that. And I certainly don't want to compromise you. I guess we have done all we can to point the police in the right direction. If they don't want to go there, I guess that is not our problem."

"Unless they start pestering you again."

"Right. OK, thanks. Don't hesitate to call me again if you want to talk more."

"You too. Ciao, Paul.

"Dasvidanya, Veronika."

PART IV: Thirteen Years Later

After my unsatisfactory phone conversations with Fred Jameson and Veronika Vlesniuk, I sat at my desk for a long time pondering what to do next. After an hour or longer of considering different scenarios I could initiate – scenarios which included another visit to Osborne, an attempt to contact Mikael Vichansky, further contact with Jameson, conversations with former Lakeside colleagues, including the head of campus security, and my friend Steve Weston – I finally decided that the wisest, most prudent course of action was to do nothing, and to wait to see what would happen next.

And nothing did. Inspector Jameson never contacted me again, and I heard a few months later that he had accepted a job with the police department in San Diego. I continued to correspond with former colleagues from Lakeside and learned that Osborne returned to work as a chemistry professor in the fall of 1999. Everyone including him seemed happy to forget the brief mental breakdown that had led him to confess to the murder of Peter White. No one talked to him about it. He talked to no one about it. He and I have never communicated with one another again.

I saw Steve Weston in the fall of 1999, a year after the murder. I joined him and his wife in New York to see a play and have dinner. We spoke briefly about White and the mystery still surrounding his death. But the conversation focused more on how much better the overall campus atmosphere was, now that White's malefic influence had been removed. And then we moved on to other topics. We have seen each other a couple of times since, and White's name didn't come up.

White's "widow" (the divorce had never been finalized) benefitted from a modest insurance policy which permitted her to open a small communications consulting business in Madison. She remarried in 2001. Her children are doing well.

Peter White gradually disappeared from everyone's consciousness. Everyone except me. I didn't really dwell on him; he was far from an obsession with me as my life evolved. I occasionally dreamed directly and indirectly about the shooting. And I found myself often returning to the questions: Had I murdered Peter White? What were the implications of that fact?

Several times following Veronika Vlesniuk's startling revelation that a bullet other than mine had perhaps shattered Peter White's head on the night of November 30, 1998, I had tried to relive that night in my mind. Could there have been another gunman in the woods with me? Had someone been stalking me? Was there someone who had guessed my intentions and my plans, who had been shadowing me, and who was there in the night with me, better armed and better skilled to commit the murder? In my recreations of the actual moment of the shooting, I recalled that the sound of the second gunshot was very different from the sound of the first. I had initially ascribed that difference to my heightened nervous sensitivity. But I had been clearly aware that the sound was louder, that there had been an echoing, and that there might have been multiple reports. That memory exploded in my mind during the dinner at Meritage with Veronika and caused my momentary malaise.

I thought often about the other gunman. I thought more about him than about Peter White. Was he some hireling of Mikael Vichansky, charged with avenging the slight done by White to the international arms traffickers? At what point had he become aware of me and my plan? Was I his unwitting accomplice? A clumsy obstacle? A useful tool? Might he have viewed my amateurish plotting and preparation as an amusement? Perhaps I had provided an unexpected but welcome diversion from what would otherwise have been a rather easy, banal day at the office. "Here is this clumsy professor trying to do the work of a professional hit man. I will entertain myself by following him and using him. If necessary, I will dispose of him, but that may not be necessary." (Obviously, it wasn't.)

I do need to correct an overstatement. I said that I waited for another development in the Peter White murder case, and that nothing happened. That is technically correct in the sense that there was no follow-up contact from the police. I did, however, eventually learn more about the details of the police investigation of the shooting, and something wonderful did emerge from all of that: I am now living in

Chicago, married to Veronika Vlesniuk. We had kept in touch in the months following the phone conversation summarized above, and in the summer of 1999, I accepted her invitation to visit her in Chicago. We continued to see each other often in the following years, until my December 2006 retirement from the Dean's position at USP gave me the freedom to move to Chicago. We were married the next month, and have lived happily together since then.

Before asking Veronika formally to accept me as her husband, I had to overcome my misgivings based on the role I had played in the death of her former lover and friend, Peter White. Those misgivings were somewhat allayed as a result of a visit I paid to the Outagamie County Sheriff's Office in the summer of 2006. As the time for my retirement approached, and it became increasingly plausible that Veronika would accept to marry me, I was overcome by a perhaps absurd longing to purge my guilt in the matter, by a crazy impulse to walk into the police department with my own version of an "It was I who..." confession. I drove to Riverdale on a Friday in August, not really sure what I would do and say.

I walked into the sheriff's office at about two p.m., and told the clerk I wanted to talk with a homicide inspector because I had some information about a 1998 murder in Lakeside. The clerk, a young woman, vaguely remembered that a professor had been murdered, but had no clear recollection of the details. But she politely took me into the back office area, and introduced me to inspector Claudia Stowe. She was a heavy-set woman of about forty, with a square jaw and what appeared to be a permanent scowl. When we were seated in her small office, I announced tentatively that I had some information about the 1998 murder of Peter White. I then told her that at the time of the investigation, I was a suspect, and had had several conversations with Inspector Frederick Jameson. She knew him vaguely.

"Yeah, I talked with Fred. He took a job in San Diego, and was already gone when I started here, but we had a couple of phone conversations about on-going matters. But I don't remember ever talking with him about the White murder."

"That's surprising. He was the lead investigator in that case, and it was still unsolved when he went off."

"Let me see if I can find the file." She was gone a very long time, and finally came back with a thick manila folder.

"It took me awhile, because, based on what you said, I was looking at open investigations. But this one was closed in the winter of 1999. Closed by Jameson before he left here."

"Was the murderer actually identified?"

Inspector Stowe thumbed through the file. "Yup, but never brought to trial. The murderer was Ilya Petrovich, a Russian national, associated with a gang of international arms dealers, with connections in Chicago. There is an Interpol warrant for his arrest still pending. It is assumed that he is living in Russia."

"How did Jameson track him down?"

"He obviously didn't. A lot of the documents in this file have FBI and Interpol letterhead. Surprising that Jameson never told you the investigation was closed, if, as you say, you were a suspect."

"I was never sure whether or not I was a suspect. I had a reasonable motive and no confirmable alibi, so he had to question me."

"Right, I see the notes of his conversations with you, Dean Steinman."

"Do you know what led Interpol and the FBI to the Russian?"

"Let me see if I can find that quickly... Yes, the fatal bullet was fired from a Russian sniper rifle, a Dragunov. The actual weapon was found in the woods near the scene of the crime, and traced to a Chicago gun dealer who had sold it to Ilya Petrovich."

"I had heard that other bullets might have been also found at the scene..."

"Right. Two M-1 bullets were found embedded in the cabinets. Petrovich had an accomplice, but he evidently missed the mark. That gun was later found buried in a state park, and traced to a gun dealer who had sold it at a show. Appears to be a dead end. But, tell me Dean Steinman, what brought you around here today."

"I will be straightforward with you, Inspector Stowe. Several months after the murder, I had a conversation with a former girlfriend of the victim, a Ukrainian woman who seemed to have some valuable information which I reported to Jameson. He didn't seem interested, and now I know why. What you have found in the files confirms the suspicions of the Ukrainian woman, and so it appears that Jameson already knew what I had found out from her. Well, I am planning to marry that woman, and our differing relationships to the victim constituted a cloud that I wanted to dissipate. You have helped me to do that. And I thank you!"

As I left the sheriff's office, I was not completely sure how to handle the next step. It appeared that there was nothing to fear from the police, and that therefore I was completely cleared in the eyes of the law. But what about my own eyes? And, more importantly, Veronika's? I decided, as I drove back to Saint Paul, that before we talked seriously about marriage, I needed to be completely honest with her about my intentions and my actions on that night in November of 1998. We were planning to get together the following weekend in Chicago, and I decided to take advantage of that opportunity to tell her everything, and then propose marriage if she was willing to accept as her husband the man who had tried unsuccessfully to murder her former fiancé.

When we spoke mid-week, she offered to make dinner for the two of us Friday night, as I would be arriving pretty late after the six hour drive from the Twin Cities. I eagerly accepted. When I arrived, about nine p.m., she had a Stoli martini waiting for me. For about fifteen minutes we talked about everyday mundane concerns, our jobs, my trip, world affairs. And then with the martini warming my body and my brain, I delicately began my confession.

"Veronika, my dear, I need to tell you something about myself that I have never told anyone."

"Uh oh! This sounds scary."

"Well, in fact, it really is scary to me, because when I tell you this, you may never want to see me again, and that would be the worst thing that ever happened to me."

"Worse than the death of your wife?"

"Yes, I didn't cause her to die, I am blameless for that terrible misfortune. If I lose you, it is because of who I am and what I did."

"You had better tell me quickly what you have done that is so terrible."

"I shot Peter White."

"That is ridiculous, Paul. I know for a fact that it was a gunman hired by Mikael Vichansky who shot Peter White."

"What you don't know is that I was in the woods outside his apartment too, and shot two bullets from my M-1 rifle that were directed at White's head, but apparently I missed."

"That is crazy, impossible!"

"Crazy maybe. But certainly possible. I had driven down to Lakeside after work that evening, and was in the woods outside Peter's kitchen window at eleven-thirty, intending to kill him. I never imagined there was anyone else around. The first time I learned that someone else might have been there was the night we first met, when you told me that the bullet from a Russian rifle had been found at the scene."

"Until that moment, you thought you had killed him?"

"Yes, in fact I thought so until just last week! I shot once and missed. As I fired the second shot, the initial sound, and then the reverberations, which seemed to echo and persist, surprised me, but it never occurred to me that the sound was from a second shooter in the woods with me. It was just six days ago that I had confirmation from an inspector with the Riverdale police that my two M-1 bullets were found in the cabinets behind where Peter stood, and that the bullet that shattered his head was from a Russian sniper rifle."

"OK. OK. So, let's say that I believe you were in the woods that night shooting at Peter. But there is still so much that doesn't make sense. Were you going to let the poor chemistry professor who confessed be executed for your crime? And, hadn't you already left the Lakeside Campus for Saint Paul at the time of the shooting? What the hell were you trying to kill him for, when you didn't even work there anymore?"

There were astonishment and disbelief in her tone and words, but no anger or blame. I was encouraged.

"You may not want to believe this, Veronika, but I did it for the others."

"The others?"

"My faculty and staff friends at the Lakeside Campus, who for over ten years had suffered from Peter White's poisonous presence. And for the students who in the next ten years would be spared the bullying negativity of a narcissistic mad man."

"Really? But you were willing to let one of those faculty friends go to jail."

"I went to visit Larry Osborne in his prison cell after he confessed. He told me he knew I had done it, and had confessed to some extent to protect me."

"What? Why did he think you had done it?"

"He lives not far from Peter's apartment. A couple of nights in the last summer I was still working at the campus, I had scouted out White's apartment late at night, and on one of those nights Osborne happened to be out walking his dog, and saw me. He guessed then what I was plotting, and approved."

"Would you have let him be convicted?"

"No. Even though he urged me to. But I learned quickly afterwards that the police didn't believe his confession."

"So you were willing to commit a murder solely to solve the Peter White problem at the Lakeside Campus"?

"There is a little more to it."

"What more?" (Said with a slight smile at the corner of her lips.)

"Because I was sure I could get away with it."

"You saw yourself as the perpetrator of the perfect crime."

"In a sense, yes, though I was aware of some imperfections in my scheme; I had no confirmable alibi, and the gun was potentially traceable to me. I have to admit that I was also attracted by a couple of literary antecedents to my crime, Dostoyevsky's Raskolnikov, and Gide's Lafcadio."

"I see. Does that make me your Sonya? Am I to follow you to your Siberian prison after you confess? Don't count on that, Mr. Raskolnikov!" And then, after a pause, "Fucking men!"

"What?"

"You heard me. You fucking men think you can solve personal problems with a gun, and the problems of the world with wars that make the world a lot worse off."

"I agree that that is true of the present war in Iraq, but I think you will agree with me that going after Hitler was maybe a good idea. And remember that Golda Meir, Indira Gandhi and Margaret Thatcher all led their nations into war. And don't forget Lady Macbeth!"

"I suppose I have to agree that there are thoughtful and necessary reasons to go to war, and those courageous women did what they had to. But I hope you don't buy the argument that Lady Macbeth pushed her unwilling husband to commit murder. Remember, that is what he was famous for: fighting and slaughtering. He was a bit reluctant when it came to killing a fellow tribesman, and I find that hypocritical. Lady Macbeth knew who he was and what he was capable of. But let's get back to you. How do you feel about what you did?"

"Good question. Certainly conflicted, but not really overwhelmed with guilt or remorse. I went into this thoughtfully and altruistically. I felt I could make one small corner of the world a better place by an act that put me at some risk, and that was ultimately 'prejudicial' to one individual whom I am thoroughly convinced was unredeemably evil. The results are satisfying; not only is the campus a better place, but I am also a happier man, as I met you through this, and we might not have met if I had not tried to shoot Peter. Though I am at this moment concerned that I might lose your love and respect, as a result of what I did."

"You have lost neither my love nor my respect. I am shaken by what you have told me. There is in you a vast region that I never suspected could exist, a man of action, a secretive schemer, a decisive man capable of strong feeling and boldness, but also capable of manipulative behavior and subterfuge. I am pleased with your openness in telling me this, and I need reassurance that you will always tell me everything that you are thinking and planning. I want no more surprises."

"Thank you, Veronika, you have my word. If I could go back in time, I don't think I would do it again, that is, try to murder Peter White. I was not sorry to see that my deed seemed to have had the desired effect of turning what had been a demoralized and dysfunctional campus into a much happier place. But the toll on me has been a lot heavier than I had anticipated. At first I enjoyed the game of cat and mouse I had to play with Inspector Jameson, but it became stressful. Deceit does not come naturally to me, and I was forced to lie to him, and to many other people, people whom I care about, and who respected and trusted me. That betrayal still weighs on me. I just have to accept that I did what I did, and therefore I am who I am, a man who was capable of plotting and carrying out a brutal crime against another man, and of lying to people he cared about. I can't change that."

"And as for the game of cat and mouse, in the end, Jameson won. He never arrested me, but wherever he is, I am sure he knows that I was in the woods that night with my rifle, trying to kill Peter White. That he knows this and still never tried to get me arrested is a bit humiliating."

"Are you at all tempted to tell your story as a redemptive act?"

"I have thought about that. I know from TV crime shows that there is no statute of limitations on murder, but I bet there is for attempted murder. After eight years, it is likely I could tell the story and face no legal consequences; I imagine they can no longer prosecute me, but I would want to get the advice of a lawyer."

"André Gide in *The Vatican Caves* has one of his characters, a novelist, point out that a fiction writer can correct – perfect – events to his liking, but in real life, there is no way to correct what we have done. We have only the old-fashioned recourse to redemption through confession and atonement. So, as you suggest, perhaps a literary confession may be a way of purging my guilt, explaining what I did and why, clearing the air. And as far as my Lakeside friends are concerned, the people for whom I tried to murder Peter, I think they would applaud me for the act, like Larry Osborne did from the start. On the other hand, my former USP colleagues would be horrified to discover that one of my methods for dealing with difficult faculty members was to station myself outside their kitchen windows with an M-1 carbine, and to attempt to solve the problem by splattering their brains on the cabinet behind them."

"As far as I know, you have never brought that particular method to bear on any of your USP colleagues?"

"No, never even tempted."

"No difficult colleagues?"

"Oh, some were testy, but certainly no matches for Pete White. He may be unique in all of academia. In fact, I can't help wondering to what extent the campus bred and nurtured his particular form of insanity. It may have been the only place in the world where he could have survived as long as he did."

"You mean some dean might have shot him sooner on another campus?"

"No, but more serious review processes would have, in most places, uncovered his deceptions, and most places would not have tolerated his manipulations. I wonder if he could have gotten tenure anywhere else. You were probably not aware, by the way, that in the midst of one of his lawsuits, he did agree to drop the suit and resign. All he wanted in exchange for going away quietly was a million dollars."

"Might have been worth it."

"If the university was ever tempted, they should thank me for trying to save them the money."

"If you do tell your story, will you tell it factually, and keep the original names?"

"No, I will probably have to change names and places, 'to protect the innocent,' as they say. To protect the guilty too. I would turn it into a fiction, a *roman à clef*. People who know me well, or who know Peter White or who are familiar with the Lakeside Campus will still recognize everything. As I said, his story is pretty unique. He took narcissism, manipulation and audacity to levels that few faculty members could aspire to. I would want, as much as possible, to use White's own words to paint his portrait. That should be the focus of the story. I would want it to be about him, and not about me. The framework of the story would have to be my murder attempt. But really, that is pretty ordinary, pretty banal. On the other hand, Peter. . . In his own words, wow! I would expect there to emerge the portrait of a uniquely maniacal character who, on a very small stage, with a limited audience, managed to demonstrate remarkable degrees of megalomania. One can easily imagine him on a larger stage, with a larger audience, successfully manipulating masses of people; he could have been a real life force to reckon with."

"I guess the world should be grateful he chose mathematics and an academic career."

As the evening wore on, the tension between us decreased. We continued for several hours talking about Peter White and me. I told her much more than I had ever told anyone about White, what he had done, and how pervasive his influence had been. She eagerly listened to my stories about White, a man who had charmed her at their first meeting, but whom she had subsequently found to be egotistical, manipulative, irresponsible, and ruthless.

I also told her a lot more about me, focusing on my thoughts and actions in preparation for the attempted murder, and then the ordeal of the investigation. I further elaborated that one of my role models for the murder was Gide's protagonist Lafcadio Wluiki, who inherits a large sum of money and, while experiencing the resulting sense of total freedom, commits a motiveless crime, just because he feels like it and knows he can get away with it. I discovered however, later, upon rereading the novel, that Lafcadio, through the act of expending his freedom, loses it. The novel leaves open the question whether or not he will confess, but, increasingly bound by unforeseen contingencies beyond his control, Lafcadio is overwhelmed by feelings of regret. He is tempted, like my other literary antecedent, Raskolnikov, to seek redemption through confession, and is urged on by a woman who loves him.

As I retold the story, she marveled at my naiveté, admired the selflessness of Larry Osborne's confession, and the tenacity and cleverness of Inspector Jameson. Ultimately, she seemed to understand and even condone what I had done. From our conversation of that evening came the inspiration for this narrative. It is a story that I do not tell with pride. While my intention may have been self-sacrificing and, in some eyes, noble, the project was cruel, and contrary to a principle in which I believe. "Thou shalt not kill." Not even Peter White. In my role as murderer, I was forced to lie, conceal, and manipulate facts, acts which I do not condone or excuse. I betrayed the trust of friends. The thin mantle of intellectual and moral superiority which I tried to wrap around my shoulders proved threadbare. I behaved like a common criminal, and was saved from a morally heinous crime only because of my ineptness.

And so, approximately six months ago, I sat down at my computer and began the task of recreating the events and my state of mind of November 30, 1998. I still had in my files the transcripts of my deposition and the depositions of others taken in preparation for the Peter White lawsuit jury trial, and I quickly realized that they offered insights into White's personality and behavior which were far more penetrating than my meager literary skills could produce. So I decided to quote from them extensively, with only minor editorial changes.

I believe I have honestly traced my motivation and my actions of that day, and then my reactions as the unforeseeable consequences developed. I allow readers of this tale to draw their own moral conclusions. I have already expressed my regrets, and have no intention of dwelling on them any further. I did what I did. I was who I was. I have moved on.

APPENDIX
From the Journal of Frederick Jameson

They brought me in this afternoon the preliminary ballistic report from the Peter White shooting. Three bullets were extracted from the wooden cabinets behind where the victim was standing, two from an M-1 carbine, the third from a Dragunov. It appeared that the Dragunov bullet had passed fatally through the victim's left temporal lobe; the two M-1s were clean misses. The Dragunov bullet is from the rifle left at the scene, seventy-five yards from the kitchen window through which the bullets had passed. No sign of the M-1; the M-1 bullets were fired from a different angle and from closer range.

So, what happened here? A guy misses twice with his M-1, and while the victim waits patiently, he puts the rifle away, pulls out his Dragunov, moves up the hill, and from there hits him squarely in the left temple? No, must have been two or even three shooters. No more than two, as the two M-1 bullets are from the same gun. So, we have one deadly accurate Russian, and then the M-1 guy who misses twice from closer range. Why did they send the M-1 guy at all? Does he shoot twice, miss both times, and so the Russian takes over?

It appears that the two shooters are pretty far apart from each other, with the Russian up higher, so if they are communicating, it must be by signs. Maybe the communication gets screwed up. The M-1 guy is closer. He shoots and misses, and White is still standing there, so the Russian decides to take over. But the M-1 guy doesn't get the signal, and they both shoot at once, with the M-1 guy missing again. Something like that. What about this M-1 guy? The Russian posts him closer to the target, with a better, straighter angle, and he misses twice. Why is the Russian working with this guy? What am I missing here?

While I am still waiting for the FBI to get back to me with the registration information on the Dragunov – and I don't know why it is taking them more than two weeks, unless they have the information and don't want to share it with country bumpkin police inspector Jameson – I have been spending a lot of time continuing my investigation of potential local – and one not so local – suspects.

I have just returned from a trip to the Twin Cities, where I interviewed the not so local guy, Dr. Paul Steinman. He was the academic dean at the Lakeside Campus for seven years, long enough to build up a strong hatred for Peter White. However, he seemed to believe sincerely that he didn't hate the guy and tried hard to convince me that he didn't hate him or wish him ill, but then everything he said made it sound like he did hate him, and is glad he is dead. Steinman kept saying things like that White was "too offensive," "too difficult," "annoying," "rude," and "unreasonable." But would that lead a man who has everything to lose and nothing to gain to the decision to commit a murder? He has nothing to gain because four months before the murder, he left the Lakeside Campus for the University of Saint Paul, after which he would never again have to deal with White.

He is pretty clever. He subtly managed to get me thinking about another of the local suspects I had somewhat overlooked, a chemistry professor named Larry Osborne. Steinman has no confirmable alibi. He handled that without any defensiveness, but it was a bit staged. His calendar that he needed to consult was conveniently placed, and his reading of it was a bit too easy and eager. It sounded rehearsed. And then his little story about recent experience skeet shooting sounded a bit too cute and rehearsed also. It is of course perfectly normal for an innocent man who knows he may be a suspect to rehearse his answers. And the fact that he has no confirmable alibi is not unusual for a man who lives alone. I would hate to have to seek confirmation of where I have spent many of my evenings.

I threw him a bit of a curveball when I asked him who was playing in the football game he said he was watching that night. Not sure why I did that, maybe just to see if he squirmed. He seemed a bit startled by the aggressiveness of the question, but his answer was correct and natural, a good answer that wasn't too good (if he had recited the exact number of passing yards Elway accumulated, that would have been too good). He was maybe well prepared for the question and seeking not to appear too well prepared.

How should I follow up with him? I'll leave him alone for a couple of weeks, and then come back at him. I should know more by then.

January 4, 1999

After the FBI got back to me last week with the information they had on the owner of the Dragunov, I was tempted to close the book on the murder of Peter White. It had been bought from a Chicago area gun dealer by a Russian national named Ilya Petrovich. His paperwork was in order; he had no police record under that name. He was in the US on a temporary visa, and had explained to the dealer that he had inherited a ton of money from an uncle in the oil business, and was touring the US with the intention of doing a lot of hunting, and for that, he claimed, nothing could beat a Russian Dragunov. The FBI dug further and found that the guy was well documented with Interpol, that he circles the globe under several identities providing muscle in support of a group of international arms dealers. The FBI is still looking into Peter White's connection with Petrovich and friends, but they made it clear to me that the investigation is no longer in my hands, that I might as well go back to chasing underage college drinkers and investigating hunting violations, which is what they think are the only crimes we encounter in rural Wisconsin.

Yeah, but... What about the M-1 guy? Am I supposed to conclude that Petrovich recruited as an assistant a guy with an M-1, who couldn't come close to a target – he apparently missed by about two feet from fifty yards twice?

After narrowing the estimated time of the shooting, I finished my interviews with the suspects, and found that all but two – Larry Osborne and Paul Steinman – had confirmable alibis. I decided then to confront Steinman again, to pick a bit at his motivation, and to let him know that the narrower time frame put his activities of the evening of November 30 in a new light. I called him this morning, and told him I wanted to see him tomorrow.

January 5, 1999

Very intriguing conversation with Steinman! I hit him with some of the more aggressive approaches in our arsenal, and he proved very vulnerable.

I couldn't help but notice his pulse rate quicken when I asked him if he had ever been to Peter White's house. I phrased it more innocently, did he know where White lived. He told me he did not, in the most natural of tones, but there was a perceptible change in his skin tone. Touché, Paul Steinman.

I handled very gently the information about the new estimated time of death. I didn't expect him to be surprised, and he wasn't. And then I elaborated for him this fictitious analysis of profiles of potential murderers. I had reasoned that if he had indeed tried to murder Peter White, it had to be from an altruistic motivation, the desire to right wrongs, and help out his former colleagues by killing the rotten apple in their barrel. He seemed genuinely surprised – and rightly so – that the police routinely looked for Good Samaritan murderers.

Steinman handled himself pretty well, but I kept him off guard by alternating potentially alarming suggestions with expressions of confidence in his innocence. In the end, I had rattled him enough that he let his well-conceived defenses slip when I asked to look at his computer files. I put the request into the context that if indeed the files had been written during that evening, all of my suspicions would disappear. He bought that, and proceeded to give me a perfect demonstration of his innocence. Much too perfect. He had obviously rehearsed the whole process of finding the Word files on Windows Explorer, and demonstrating the time stamps on the six files written over very regular forty to forty-five minute intervals between seven and eleven p.m. on the night of the murder. I pretended to be convinced. I was in fact convinced that Steinman had manipulated the time stamp on those files to give himself an alibi.

January 8, 1999

I almost laughed at Larry Osborne when he came into my office and said he did it. He had called me in the morning to ask if he could meet with me, said he had some important information about the White case. I had to pretend to take him seriously, even though it was so far from what I was expecting, and what I was thinking, and so unlikely. But when he took me to the exact spot where the M-1 guy had been stationed, well… how could he know that? None of the ballistic information had gotten out. In fact, no one knows besides me and the FBI that there were two shooters; that has all been kept under wraps.

So, with some distaste, I had Osborne locked up. He seemed quite satisfied. We pretended to accept his version of the shooting, even though he apparently knows nothing about the Russian, and his story about using his father's old hunting rifle and dissolving it in acid was pretty far-fetched.

There is still little doubt in my mind that the M-1 guy is Steinman, and I wonder how he will respond to Osborne's confession. I have little proof at this point. I do have a 50% ID of Steinman as the Abbotsford Samaritan. That was a lucky guess. When Ryan Everson first told me about the mysterious rescuer who on the night of the White murder had saved Daniel Goodwin from the wreck of his oil tanker just before it caught fire, I had briefly entertained the idea that there might be some connection. After having met with Steinman the second time, I decided to follow up on that hunch, took a photo of Steinman from the USP website, and showed it to Goodwin and the three people who got to the scene as the Samaritan walked off. No one could say for sure, but both Goodwin himself and Brenda Groven thought it was probably the guy.

The next day, I did a lot of heavy legwork, taking Steinman's picture to show at gas stations and restaurants around the highway exits between Abbotsford and Lakeside. A server at the IHOP in Waupaca was pretty sure he was the crossword puzzle guy she had seen during her late shift that Monday night.

January 17, 1999

It's late, and I just got back from having dinner with Edward Wilson, but I wanted to jot down some notes about what has been going on in the last two days before going to bed.

I had asked the prison to let me know when Osborne had visitors, and, fortunately, I was on duty yesterday afternoon when they called to say a guy named Paul Steinman had come to see Larry Osborne! I went over to the prison and waited for him to come out. I decided I would tail him for a while, thinking just maybe I would learn something useful. I had to sit outside the prison for thirty minutes then at the Dunkin' Donut for an hour while he chatted with someone inside, but after that my patience was amply rewarded when he went out of his way to visit the spot at the entrance to Brown Creek State Park where the construction crew had dug up the M-1. Bingo!

Today, I went back to the prison to study the video tapes of Steinman's meeting with Osborne. There is no audio of course, and the videos could never be considered admissible, but I thought I might learn something useful. The cameras aren't clear enough so I could read lips, but I think I understood a lot of the body language and facial expressions. Osborne at first appeared to be mockingly condescending. I could easily imagine him saying something like, "Don't worry, Paul, I am not going to tell them what really happened that night." I saw admiration and something like affection on his face at times too. Steinman appeared shell-shocked but doing his best to hide it. I also saw admiration and affection on his face, probably at Osborne's willingness to take the rap for him. I wouldn't have expected Steinman to let Osborne into his confidence. He either needed Osborne's help, or maybe Osborne just found out somehow. Maybe he was out there that night too! But then, he would have known about the Russian.

I frequently talk shop with Edward. His work in the areas of social biology and evolutionary theory has on occasion shed some light on criminal behavior. Early on, I had decided this case was interesting enough to get some input from him, and maybe even some advice. I had previously described to him the murder scene, had read to him some excerpts from White's deposition, and told him of the FBI's conclusions and my own suspicions regarding Paul Steinman. He was intrigued by it all. He had concluded that White's combination of passive/aggressive and narcissistic personality disorders in a man with strong mathematical reasoning abilities was particularly dangerous. That he was also a bully, a cheat, and a man devoid of moral principle in his pursuit of material gratification made him even more despicable. "Who wouldn't want to bump off the son of a bitch?" was Edward's scientific assessment.

When I told him at dinner that I was now convinced that Paul Steinman was the Abbotsford Samaritan, he uttered what sounded like a shout of triumph. In response to my quizzical look, he laughed, and exclaimed, "So, your bold, determined, meticulous murderer, having formulated a clever plan to carry out his bloody deed and remain undetected, interrupts his carefully conceived scenario to rush to the rescue of a man he does not know. He risks his life to pull a complete stranger from the burning wreckage of his truck, and, in so doing, he compromises his project, and opens up the possibility that he will later be identified as being in the vicinity of the crime."

"Does that sound unlikely to you?"

"On the contrary, it is perfectly consistent with what you have told me concerning Steinman's motivation; and, for me personally, *this provides one more piece of evidence in support of the argument that instinct evolved by natural selection, and that the Haldane theory of 'inclusive fitness' just doesn't describe how people behave."*

"Can you explain that to me?"

"I think so. Back in the 50s, a British biologist named J.B.S. Haldane outlined a theory that altruism will increase in frequency in a population if the benefit to the recipient of the altruism multiplied by the kinship of the recipient to the altruist is greater than the cost to the altruist. Haldane described a scenario in which a person possessing the altruism gene sees a child in danger of drowning in a flooded river. If there is a ten percent chance that the altruist will die in the rescue attempt and the altruism gene thereby lost, the potential altruist will only attempt the rescue if the child is closely enough related so that the altruism gene is also likely to be present in the child, and therefore perpetuated. In other words, people are more likely to be altruistic towards their blood relations. But if what you say about Steinman is true, it flies in the face of the theory of inclusive fitness, and supports my own beliefs."

"And how do you prefer to understand altruism?"

"In Darwinian terms, as a result of natural selection – but at the group, rather than the individual level. The altruism instinct in Steinman appears to be so strong that he risks his life in the short term, he compromises his project to murder White, and ultimately takes the chance of losing his liberty if he is later identified, in order to save the life of a stranger, who is nonetheless a member of his group, understood as all of humanity."

"Do you think that Steinman took the time to debate whether the stranger's life was important enough to risk all of that?"

"Altruism is an inherited instinct. Actually, what is inherited is an "epigenetic rule," a propensity towards altruism, with specific altruistic behaviors learned through life experiences. Altruistic acts do not come from a rational calculation on the part of the altruist. He may consider the ultimate impact on himself, but authentic altruism is based on a biological instinct for the common good of the tribe. It results from natural selection which permitted groups of altruists in prehistoric times to prevail over groups of individuals in selfish disarray. It is possible Steinman took the time to allow his more selfish – individualistic – instinct for self-preservation to enter into debate, but that instinct was clearly weaker in him, and quickly overcome. Self-preservation was able to assert itself only

when Steinman was certain the truck driver was out of danger, and he then slipped away."

"So Steinman saves a life on his way to taking one?"

"This sounds contradictory, but genetically I think this is very consistent with what you have told me about Steinman's motivation for killing White."

"Which was also altruistic."

"The study of natural selection suggests that the first stage in the development of social behavior in any species is motivated by the desire to defend a nest against enemies. At the most primitive level, the murder of White was a protection of the nest environment of the Lakeside Campus. The crucial difference between human cognition and that of other social animals is the ability to collaborate for the purpose of achieving shared goals and intentions. White's narcissism constantly threatened shared purposes. Recent research has focused on the evolution of cooperation, and one of the human responses that developed early was the impulse to volunteer punishment and retribution for those who deviate from the norms of the group."

"It is interesting that you would tell me that. In one of my conversations with Steinman, I talked about murderer profiling, and I suggested to him that he might fit into the category of vigilante vengeance, never guessing that there was any scientific basis for it."

"Oh, yes. We are programmed to receive pleasure not only from seeing punishment meted out to those who do not cooperate; we are also motivated to take part in administering justice. We yell at motorists who disobey traffic rules, blow the whistle on cheaters, and report crimes we might see being committed. So, are you ready to arrest Steinman?"

"If I get a positive ID from the gun seller, I don't think I have that much choice. All of the evidence is circumstantial, but there is a lot of it."

"What is he technically guilty of?"

"Attempted murder."

"I guess he technically is, but…"

"But..?"

"His only goal was to rid a very nice little academic community of a man who bullied his colleagues, his supervisors, and, worst of all, his students, a man who shamelessly sold his mathematical knowledge to illegal arms dealers for distribution to mercenaries, assassins and terrorists. As you yourself told me, Steinman had nothing to gain from this beyond the satisfaction of freeing the Lakeside Campus,

and for that matter the whole world, of the very negative influence of a very bad man. That altruist will go to jail, while the real arms dealing murderers who actually killed him go free?"

"Steinman broke the law, Edward. It is my duty to investigate crimes, and then report the results of my investigation. The clear result is that Paul Steinman attempted to murder Peter White."

"Weren't you told by the FBI to stay out of this?"

"Yes, and no. They made it clear that I was not to continue my investigation into the Russian sniper who actually killed White. But there is no reason why I can't pursue the M-1 guy whom I know to be Paul Steinman."

"If no one knows anything about the Russian, does Steinman still think that he murdered Peter White?"

"As far as I know."

"How can he not know that the Russian was also there shooting at White?"

"That is strange, but plausible. When I first understood there were two shooters, I assumed they were working together, and that puzzled me. Why would a Russian pro cooperate with a local amateur? My present recreation of the crime scene has the two shooters in the woods, seventy-five yards apart, with the Russian up on a hill, above and to the north of Steinman's position. The Russian can see into the kitchen window seventy-five yards below him, and can also see Steinman, below and to his right, about seventy-five yards from the Russian, and fifty yards from the window. He is watching both Steinman and White. But Steinman does not see him. The Russian watches Steinman as he takes and misses his first shot, and then times his shot to be fired simultaneously with White's second shot, so the two reports cover each other. Steinman thinks it is his bullet that shattered White's skull."

"Why does the Russian do that?"

"He wants to make sure that White dies, but wants to avoid calling attention to his presence if possible."

"Did the Russian know that Steinman was going to be there?"

"My guess is that he didn't. It is an unlikely coincidence, to be sure, that both gunmen appeared on the same night. But that coincidence is the more reasonable conclusion. The organization the Russian works for would not have known what Steinman was plotting. The Russian probably got there first, was surprised, maybe annoyed, maybe amused to see this other guy plant himself in front of

the window, and he worked around him. Probably good for Steinman that he wasn't blocking the Russian's line of fire!"

"So, Steinman is just a potential fly in the ointment?"

"Yup."

"So, will you really arrest a potential fly for attempted murder?"

"I don't know. Let's see how this develops. I still need a positive ID from the gun seller in Menomonie to be 100% sure. Then I will confront Steinman one more time. To me, the best outcome would be for Steinman to step forward, confess, and let the DA's office decide what charges to press."

"That way, you get to wash your hands of the matter."

"I am really torn here, Edward! I get your point. Yes, Steinman is a good man, a man we can admire, whose motives we identify with and approve, a man who commits a crime for all the right reasons, a man whose gene pool we would like to see perpetuated! Throughout his rather pitiful murder attempt, he was woefully inept, outmaneuvered, and lost among complex interests and events he did not begin to comprehend. But I am a police officer with responsibilities. I investigate crimes, and report my findings to our prosecutors so that the judicial system can review the facts and punish, exonerate or pardon. It is a good, fair system. And I am sworn to respect it."

"Even though a higher authority, the FBI, has warned you off?"

"That is something to keep in mind. Let's see how this develops."

January 21, 1999

I have just come back from my third visit to see Paul Steinman in Saint Paul. The guy might be thinking I have a crush on him! Actually, I think I made him quite uncomfortable, and that was exactly my intention. He never really squirmed, but there were telltale color changes.

I had arranged to stop on my way up to see him to talk with the guy in Menomonie who had sold the M-1 they dug up in the park. When I talked with him on the phone, he said he had sold it last summer, but didn't remember much about the buyer. But I thought a personal visit might make an impression. It did. Funny how gun sellers suddenly get cooperative when you let them know that one of their guns was involved in a felony. I showed him Steinman's picture and he said he was 80% sure that he was the guy who had purchased the M-1; he even said he would be willing to testify.

After that, I felt I really had little more to learn from Dr. Steinman. I looked on it as a courtesy call through which I hoped to let him know subtly that I had the goods on him.

Did it never really occur to the guy that I might have read Crime and Punishment? I know about his Columbia and Yale degrees, but cops go to school too! Even if it is only the University of Wisconsin. At any rate, I was more amused than annoyed by the little scene he had set up for my arrival in his office, with Steinman and his secretary laughing gaily at some joke they had shared, and which I recognized as an adaptation of a ploy Raskolnikov uses.

Much of his forced gaiety disappeared when I let him know that I had viewed the video tapes of his conversation with Osborne. Then, to let him know that we had found the rifle and traced it to him, I decided on the spot to try my hand at a little Dostoyevskian subterfuge, and created a context in which to ask him if he was aware of the construction going on at Brown Creek State Park. I know I got him with that one! Then I tried to raise his paranoia level even higher by making it appear that I was surreptitiously attempting to get his fingerprints by taking his map. He should be thoroughly shaken. I have left the door wide open for him to follow up, but I don't think he will.

January 25, 1999

When Steinman called me this morning, I got a little excited: maybe he was going to step up and confess. But then, no... I never imagined he would get together with Veronika Vlesniuk, and that she would tell him what she knew about the Russians. I didn't know how much she really knew, as the FBI wouldn't let me go back and question her a second time. Apparently she knows a lot. At any rate, it must have been a strange meeting between the former fiancée of the murder victim and the guy who thought he had killed him!

I showed no interest in what Steinman called to tell me. He must have been very disappointed. If you want to get my attention, Dr. Steinman, pay me a little respect and tell me the truth! In fact, I am tired of this cat and mouse game, and with the move to San Diego now a certainty, I have to decide in the next week what I am going to do about the White murder case.

I would have loved to have seen Steinman's face when she told him that he was not alone in the woods that night, and that he did not kill Peter White. Did he let on to her that he thought he was the killer? I bet not. The revelation that he was not alone in the woods must have shaken him to his core. Did he not realize that White's nefarious influence went far beyond the borders of the Lakeside Campus, and invited intervention by actors outside the geographic, professional and social sphere of the campus?

Steinman is a highly intelligent and highly altruistic man. He had obviously thought long and hard about the White problem, and concluded that his intervention was required, that the problem he was solving was local and contained, and that he was uniquely suited and positioned to resolve it. Convinced that both the problem and the solution belonged to him and to him alone, he conceived and carried out a bold, ingenious plan of action, and reinvented himself in the process. The genial professor and dean emerged as a murderous – albeit altruistic – vigilante. I suspect he took pleasure in that identity, probably took pleasure too in dueling me. But he is undoubtedly torn between his conception of morality on the individual level and the collective social imperative that had spurred him to action. He will not achieve peace of mind until he learns that the tension between individual and group morality is hardwired into our genetic makeup, and that modern consciousness requires that he accept with equanimity that his deed is both good and evil.

Should I take Edward's advice and leave the guy alone, allowing him to go on propagating his strong altruistic gene, never free however from the internal confusion that will continue to trouble him? Might as well…